CARMODY'S RUN

CARMODY'S RUN

BILL PRONZINI

DARK HARVEST
Arlington Hts., Illinois · 1993

ISBN 0-913165-72-7

CARMODY'S RUN Copyright ©1992 by Bill Pronzini

Cover Artwork Copyright ©1992 by Nikita Tkachuk

ACKNOWLEDGEMENTS:

"Preface: On Carmody and the Writing Life"
  Copyright ©1992 by Bill Pronzini.
"The Desperate Ones" Copyright ©1971 by H.S.D.
  Publications, Inc. Originally published in *Alfred
  Hitchcock's Mystery Magazine*. Revised version
  Copyright ©1992 by Bill Pronzini.
"Death Warrant" Copyright ©1972 by H.S.D. Publications,
  Inc. Originally published in *Alfred Hitchcock's Mystery
  Magazine* under the title "The Web." Revised version
  copyright ©1992 by Bill Pronzini.
"Blood Money" Copyright ©1975 by H.S.D. Publications,
  Inc. Originally published in *Alfred Hitchcock's Mystery
  Magazine* under the title "Free-Lance Operation."
  Revised version Copyright ©1992 by Bill Pronzini.
A Run in Diamonds Copyright ©1973 by Alex Saxon.
  Originally published by Pocket Books under the
  pseudonym Alex Saxon. Revised version Copyright
  ©1992 by Bill Pronzini.

Manufactured in the United States of America

FIRST EDITION

Dark Harvest/P. O. Box 941/Arlington Heights, IL/60006

The publishers would like to express their gratitude to the
following people. Thank you: Ann Cameron Mikol, Stan
and Phyllis Mikol, Dr. Stan Gurnick PhD, Greg MacIntyre,
Raymond, Teresa and Mark Stadalsky, Linda and Nikita
Tkachuk, Tom Pas, Ed Gorman; and, of course, a special
thanks to Bill Pronzini.

- Table of Contents -

PREFACE:

ON CARMODY AND THE WRITING LIFE

Jack Woodford, the wacky bard of commercial writers, called us "fiction racketeers." He didn't mean hacks; he meant prolific professionals who care about their work and attempt to write to the best of their abilities at all times. There's a damn big difference between being prolific and being a hack, whether the critics and literateurs think so or not, and I'll be glad to debate the point with holders of the opposing view.

Anyhow, I've been one of the racketeers for more than a quarter of a century—twenty-seven years, to be exact. During that time I've published seven or eight million words, and lived a great many different lives while I was writing them. Some briefly, some not so briefly. Some concurrently with others. And some I'm still living to this day. There are times when I feel schizophrenic as hell. Like Sybil, except that I'm aware of each of my multiple personalities, good and bad, past and present.

I refer, of course, to the hundreds of fictional characters I've created. A clutch have been in my own image, to one degree or another; most haven't been. All have been interesting, at least to me. (The God game. Writers get off on playing it, too; don't let any of them tell you otherwise.) A few of my created lives have been so enjoyable to lead that I've brought them back for encore performances— so often in one case that the character is better known and more well-liked than I am, and he doesn't even have a name!

The San Francisco private investigator dubbed the "Nameless Detective"—by a former editor, not by me—is certainly my best as well as best known series character, having appeared in twenty novels and three-score short stories since 1967. But he's not the only one by any means. The rest, brainchildren of the seventies and eighties, have had short public existences—and languished in relative obscurity while they and I were living them.

There was Dan Connell, ex-pilot and reformed smuggler operating in Singapore and Malaysia, featured in a pair of novels, *The Jade Figurine* and *Dead Run*, originally published under the pseudonym Jack Foxx. There was Flagg, troubleshooter for a mythical criminal boss in San Francisco, a joint creation with Jeff Wallmann: hero/antihero of four shorts and one novel, *Day of the Moon*, all published as by William Jeffrey. There was Christopher Steele, magician extraordinary, who specialized in solving impossible crimes—another joint creation, this time with Michael Kurland. There was Fergus O'Hara, a seriocomic 1860s con man, who with his wife Hattie solves a riverboat mystery in another Jack Foxx opus, *Freebooty*. There was E.L. Oxman, a contemporary New York City police detective; John Lutz and I created him jointly for *The Eye*, and John subsequently wrote a solo novel featuring Oxman. There was John Quincannon, another historical character who started out as a U.S. Treasury agent in the 1890s and graduated to a partnership with ex-Pinkerton op Sabina Carpenter in a San Francisco "investigative services" agency; he appears in *Quincannon*, and in a collaboration with Marcia Muller, *Beyond the Grave*.

And then there was Carmody.

Of all my obscure series characters, I have the softest spot for Carmody, the hardest edged. I've long admired the tough, terse *Black Mask* style and its various *noir* offshoots, and in the Carmody stories I came closest to capturing that same dark flavor. (Flagg, the Organization troubleshooter, is also a *noir*-styled character; but he isn't as fully realized as Carmody, doesn't have Carmody's complexity or quite the right dark taste.)

Carmody is not a detective, although like Flagg and my other Obscures, he sometimes functions in that capacity. He is "a free-lance bodyguard, a supplier of legal and extralegal services and material, with connections that reached into nearly every country in the world; he dealt with desperate men and desperate women, with profiteers and black-marketeers, with thieves and smugglers and murderers—on his terms, according to his own brand of ethics; and he thrived on the action, adventure, danger in each of the jobs he undertook."

His base of operations is the Mediterranean island of Majorca, but his work takes him all over Europe and North Africa, to such places as Algiers, Vienna, Venice, Amsterdam, and Spain's Costa del Sol. His adventures are just that—adventure stories, with emphasis on action, unusual characters and situations, exotic settings. Man stuff, in other words. Any feminist—my wife, Marcia Muller, being no exception—will no doubt dislike and disapprove of Carmody. So be it. I make no apologies for him or his creation.

He was conceived in 1970, while Majorca was *my* base of operations. (In case you're wondering, I went there with a fellow racketeer, Jeff Wallmann, to write a series of erotic novels [I love euphemisms; don't you?] for an American publisher who was based on the island. For tax purposes—his, not ours. All expenses paid. A hell of a deal for all concerned.) Antiheroes were big that year, and I had been reading and was much impressed by the Parker series by Donald Westlake writing as Richard Stark. Dan J. Marlowe was a good friend and I liked his Earl Drake series too. So why not try an antihero of my own? Not a thief like Parker or a convicted felon turned reluctant government agent like Drake . . . somebody more edge-of-the-law than outright criminal, a kind of shadow-walker . . . somebody who operated outside the U.S., in places I myself knew first-hand, had visited or wanted to visit—an antihero version of Stephen Marlowe's Chet Drum. Enter Carmody.

His debut was in a novelette I called "A Run in Diamonds" and sold to Bruce Cassiday at Popular Publications. The story appeared in the first (December 1970) of the short-lived, digest-size issues of *Adventure*. With a new title: "The $50,000 Bosom." Bruce is a fine editor and writer and a nice man but I will never forgive him for that title change. In 1972 I expanded the story into a full-length novel for Pocket Books; it was published the following year under my original title and the pseudonym Alex Saxon. It was supposed to be the first of a series of Carmody novels for Pocket. And others *would* have followed if my editor hadn't left shortly after I delivered the manuscript of *A Run in Diamonds*. Her replacement had no interest in continuing the series, and subsequent sales of *Diamonds* weren't good enough for PB's bosses to override the new editor's disinterest.

Carmody did appear in three other short stories published between 1971 and 1975, all in *Alfred Hitchcock's Mystery Magazine*. Those three stories are included in these pages. Following publication of the last of them, "Blood Money" (blandly retitled "Free-Lance Operation" by *AHMM*), I decided to see if I could interest some new and enterprising editor in Carmody as a series book character. I wrote a 50-page portion-and-outline based on "Blood Money" and sent it to my then-agent, who in turn sent it to one hardcover and half a dozen paperback houses. No takers. This type of antihero had had his day, they all said. Carmody wasn't "hardboiled" enough for the male action-adventure market, the paperback editors said. Meaning he didn't carry enough firepower or indiscriminately kill enough people; this was the heyday of The Executioner and his ilk, remember. Hell, I thought, they're probably right. So I retired the portion-and-outline and Carmody along with it, and went on to other pursuits.

I might have considered another Carmody short story at some point, just to keep a hand in, if *AHMM* hadn't been bought by Davis Publications in 1975 and its editorial policies somewhat revamped. *Noir* antihero stories were not any more in favor with the new regime than they were with paperback editors. Not that all was smooth sailing with the old *AHMM* regime. In fact, a dispute with editor Ernie Hutter was the reason I didn't write a Carmody story between 1972 and 1975.

Both "The Desperate Ones" and "Death Warrant" (magazine title: "The Web") were heavily edited, in the latter case so extensively that the published version carried little of my Vienna background description, so little that no real sense of the city and its people remained. When I complained to Ernie he said he felt the descriptions were unnecessarily detailed and besides *AHMM* "wasn't in the business of publishing travelogues." Maybe not, but I maintained—to no avail—that the background material was a vital element to the series as well as to the story; without it, "Death Warrant" might as well have been set in Podunk, Utah and Carmody might as well operate in Cincinnati. I still think I'm right. In theory, anyway.

On the other hand . . .

In those days I was still learning the craft of fiction. Which is a polite way of saying that I didn't know my ass from a simile. I like to think that I have finally, in my forties, learned at least some literary lessons fairly well. In any case I cringe when I read most of my early work. God, how I overwrote! I wanted the reader to see and hear and feel every minute detail of a scene, so I relentlessly overdescribed. I wanted to make sure the reader didn't miss a single scrap of pertinent (and not so pertinent) information, so I overexplained. I wanted to establish a distinctive "voice," which to me back then meant choosing the ornate phrase over the direct one, the fancy word over the plain one.

I was, in short, a fledgling literary putz.

Ernie Hutter was right after all. Not in theory, but at least partially in practice.

Ah, youth. Ah, hell.

The point of this little confession is that my early work cries out—no, *shrieks*—for blue-pencilling and revising. Whenever an opportunity arises to do just that, I'm quick to seize it. This volume was one of those happy opportunities. Thanks to the good folks at Dark Harvest, I've not only been able to bring Carmody and his adventures to a new group of readers, but to extensively overhaul *A Run in Diamonds* and the three short stories.

This is not to say that I've updated them. I haven't. They're very much reflective of their era, the early seventies, and of what each of the various Mediterranean, European, and North African locales was like when I knew it at the time; I felt it would be wise to let them stand in their proper historical context. (I should point out that my depiction of these places is not exaggerated in any way. Spain was still a dictatorship under Franco and Spanish justice was swift and merciless. There was almost no major crime on Majorca; nobody locked doors and everybody was at least a little afraid of running afoul of the Guardia Civil. As for Algiers, my descriptions are if anything restrained. Would you believe Carmody encountering an Arab with dirty robes hiked up around his waist, blithely taking a leak on the wall of the American consulate at high noon? No? I witnessed just such a sight myself in 1970, from a distance of about ten feet.)

Also, the plots of these stories—in particular of the three shorter ones—are too period-bound to benefit from updating. It was possible twenty years ago, in the days before international terrorism, weirdo skyjackers, and stringent airport security measures, to transport a handgun from country to country—as Carmody does—in the false bottom of a suitcase. It was also possible to travel overland with relative freedom from the Sudan through the Libyan Desert and eventually to Algiers, a point upon which part of the plot of "The Desperate Ones" turns. The ultra-high frequency radio transmitter and the purpose for which it is used in "Death Warrant" were technologically sound in 1973. The smuggling of cigarettes, as a result of the Italian government monopoly described in "Blood Money," was in fact a multimillion-dollar, cutthroat business back then.

What I *have* tried to do in revising the four Carmodys is to make them simpler, sharper, less clumsy, less cluttered, *better* stories. In the case of A *Run in Diamonds*, I've done so much cutting and revamping that it is now a reasonably effective short novel instead of a poor average-length novel. Better short and good than long and bad —a verity some of today's writers could stand to learn, eh? These new versions are also more in keeping with the *noir* tradition and my vision of what Carmody's place within it ought to be. Thus I hope they'll be of interest to readers who have met Carmody before, as well as to readers who are meeting him here for the first time.

The God game again. Not only are we writers able to create new characters out of whole cloth, we're able to resurrect old characters and reshape them into better versions of themselves and better representations of ourselves. Plus we get to live their (far more exciting than our own) lives all over again.

And I'll bet you thought we got into this business for the money . .

—Petaluma, California
May 1992

THE
DESPERATE ONES

Carmody had never liked Algiers. It was hot, over-crowded, dirty, and seemed saturated with a permanent sweet-sour stink. But the main reason was that it was full of people you couldn't trust, people who would cut your throat for a couple of dinars and smile while they were doing it.

In his room at the St. George, on the Boulevard Salah Bouakouir, he stood sourly looking out over the harbor and the Mediterranean beyond. It was washday, and every grillwork balcony on every stark-white, tile-roofed building was draped with laundry: a gigantic open-air drycleaning plant. In the hotel garden below, the palms and the olive and acacia trees had a wilted, strangulated look. Like Algiers itself, even on its best days.

Carmody turned from the window, began to pace the room—a lean, predatory man, thirty-seven years old, with flat green eyes and shaggy graying-black hair. A sardonic mouth made him appear faintly satanic. There was a vague air of brittleness about him, as if you could hurt him physically without too much effort; but his eyes told you this was a lie, that he was as hard as a block of forged steel inside.

The room was air-conditioned but he was sweating inside a thin yellow shirt and white ducks. A rum collins would have gone good about now, but he was supposed to go to work soon and he seldom drank when he worked. He glanced again at his watch. Almost four-thirty. The woman, Nicole, was late. He didn't care for people who weren't punctual, especially where business was concerned. He was not a patient man.

Carmody was a freelance bodyguard, a supplier of legal and extra-legal services and material, with connections that reached into nearly every country in the world; he dealt with desperate men and desperate women, with profiteers and black marketeers, with thieves and smugglers and murderers—on his terms, according to his own brand of ethics; and he thrived on the action, adventure, danger in each of the jobs he undertook. He worked inside the law and outside it, whichever suited the occasion, and had never failed a client or been arrested for even the most minor of offenses. It wasn't cheap, going to him, but you were guaranteed results. He was good, so good that in the shadow world in which he operated his reputation commanded the highest respect.

The job that had brought him to North Africa had to do with a quarter of a million dollars in assorted raw gems. The day before, at his villa on the island of Majorca, he had received a call from one of his contacts, an Algierian black marketeer named Achmed. Achmed had been approached by a Frenchman calling himself Paul Tobiere, the man with the gems. Tobiere had come to Algiers from the Sudan, where he had lived for several years; come by way of the Libyan Desert, Tripoli, and the coast of Tunisia. Twice en route he'd nearly been killed by former associates who wanted the stones and their ex-partner's skin as a bonus. How Tobiere had come by the gems, who the former associates were, didn't concern Carmody. What concerned him was that Tobiere was so anxious to get out of North Africa, he was willing to pay one-tenth of the gems' worth for safe passage to France and a new identity when he got there.

Contact with the Frenchman was not to be made through Achmed, as Carmody would have preferred, but through a woman Tobiere had known in the Sudan named Nicole Moreau, now a resident of Algiers. Apparently Nicole was the one providing Tobiere with his hidey hole here. He hadn't told Achmed where that was; he was too frightened to trust anyone with that knowledge, he'd said, except Carmody himself.

The meeting with Nicole had been arranged for four o'clock, but there was still no sign of the woman. Carmody would give her until five o'clock. If she hadn't showed by then, the deal was off. He didn't need $25,000 that badly. It was the work that energized him anyway, not the money he got from it.

It didn't come down to a call-off; Nicole Moreau beat the deadline by ten minutes. She was in her late twenties, tall, broad-hipped, with thick blue-black hair cropped short. Dark brooding eyes appraised him coolly as he let her into the room.

He said, "What's the idea of keeping me waiting so long?"

"I apologize, *m'sieu*. I was detained."

"Detained how?"

"With my profession."

"What profession is that?"

"I am a dancer at the Cafe Bulbul."

"Yes? Why didn't you call?"

"There was not time to use the telephone."

"What's more important, your dancing or Tobiere's life?"

She made a pouting face. "You are not very pleasant, *m'sieu*."

"I'm not paid to be pleasant. Where's Tobiere?"

"A house on the Rue Kaddour Bourkika."

"Where's that?"

"The Casbah."

"That figures," Carmody said. "He have the gems with him?"

"No."

"Did he tell you where they are?"

"No. He will tell only you."

Carmody went to the wardrobe, strapped on his Beretta in its belt half-holster. The woman watched him without expression. He donned a lightweight cotton jacket; with the bottom button fastened, the gun didn't show at all.

He said, "You drive here or come in a taxi?"

"A taxi," Nicole answered.

"Then we'll use my car."

It was in the hotel garage, a small Fiat he'd rented at the Dar-el-Beida Airport. He knew the steep, twisting streets of Algiers only slightly, so he let Nicole direct him through the congested midday traffic. They climbed one of the hills on which the city had been built, toward the basilica of Notre Dame d'Afrique on Mt. Bouzarea high above. Two-thirds of the way up Nicole veered them to the left and into the fringes of the Casbah.

It had a romantic image, the Casbah, thanks to the Pepé LeMoko nonsense, but the reality of it was anything but romantic. It was a vast, squalid slum in which eighty thousand Arabs were packed like cattle into ancient buildings sprawled along a labyrinth of narrow streets and blind alleys. It teemed with flies, heat, garbage, and vermin both animal and human. Europeans and Americans were safe enough there in the daytime, as long as they didn't venture too deep into the maze of back alleys. At night, not even Carmody would have gone there alone.

The Arabs had a saying: *Tawakkul' al' Allah.* Rely on God. If you lived in the Casbah, Carmody thought, and you weren't a thief or a cutthroat, you'd have to rely on God; you wouldn't have another choice.

The woman directed him into a bare cement plaza crowded with dark-skinned children, veiled women, old men in burnooses and striped *gallabiyyas.* It was the nearest place where a car could be parked, she said. They went on foot down the Street of Many Steps, into the bowels of the district. On the way a rag-clad beggar accosted them, asking *baksheesh*; Nicole brushed by him roughly but Carmody gave him a dinar. He reserved his cruelty for those who deserved it.

Half a dozen turns brought them into Rue Kaddour Bourkika. It was no more than three feet wide, the rough stucco walls on either side chalked and crayoned in Arabic and English, in one place marred with old bullet scars—mementoes of the French-Algerian War. They passed beneath balconies supported by wooden poles cemented in stone in the old Turkish manner—some of the buildings in the Casbah dated back to the Second Century—and went down more littered steps and finally stopped before an archway.

"Through here," Nicole said.

Carmody followed her through a tunnellike passageway adorned with mosaic tile, walking hunched over to keep from cracking his head on the low stone roof. The passage opened into a small courtyard with a waterless fountain and a half-dead pomegranate tree in its middle. Doorways opened off the courtyard, off an encircling balcony above. The air here was filled with tinny Arab music, the cries of children; the hot, sweet-sour stink, sharp in this enclosed space, made Carmody's head ache.

Nicole rapped on one of the doors beneath the balcony—three times, a five-second wait, and another three times. The man who opened up was in his late thirties, muscled, dry-faced in spite of the heat. He had long blond hair and pale features, the eyes of glacial blue. His white suit was rumpled but not unclean.

He said in English, "What took you so long?"

"Ask your friend here," Carmody said. "Are you Tobiere?"

"I am."

Carmody prodded the woman ahead of him, inside. A weak ceiling light let him see old square-cut furnishings covered with handwoven blankets. A window was open but there was no breeze and the air in there was stifling.

He said, "Let's have a look at the gems."

"I don't have them here," Tobiere said.

"No? Where are they?"

"In a safe place. Outside the city."

"How soon can you get them?"

"Tonight."

"What's wrong with right now?"

"Tonight," Nicole said. "Late tonight."

Carmody turned to her. "Are you his partner?"

"Not exactly that, m'sieu . . ."

"Then let him talk for himself."

"She's going with us to France," Tobiere said. "She won't—"

"Oh, she is?"

"Yes. She won't be ready to leave until later."

"The arrangement was for you alone."

"I know, but my plans have changed. Nicole will go with me."

"She will if you pay me another ten thousand."

"Another ten thousand—!"

"Two people are twice as much trouble as one," Carmody said. "Plus I'll have to make arrangements for a second set of papers. I should charge you double, fifty thousand."

Tobiere started to argue, but Nicole put a hand on his arm to silence him. She said, "He will pay what you ask. Thirty-five thousand American dollars."

"Is that right, Tobiere?"

"Yes. As you wish."

"What time will you be ready?" Carmody asked Nicole.

"Midnight, perhaps a little sooner."

"All right. We don't leave from here, though. I'm not coming back here after dark. Pick another place."

"Your hotel?" Nicole said.

"Too public. This place where you dance—the Cafe Bulbul. How about there?"

"Yes, good. I live nearby."

"What's the address?"

"Rue de Marbruk. Number Eleven."

"I'll find it," Carmody said. He shifted his gaze back to Tobiere. "You'd better have the gems with you. We don't go anywhere until I get a look at them."

"I will have them," Tobiere promised.

Carmody went to the door. "You coming with me or staying here?" he asked the woman.

"I will stay."

"Suit yourself."

He left them, returned to the Rue Kaddour Bourkika. But instead of turning upward toward the plaza, he hurried down several more steps to the Street of the Slipper Makers. There were several open-air markets here, swarming with activity, and doorless shops of all types set into tiny niches no larger than coat closets; there was also a small open-front native bar, its tables occupied by Arabs drinking glasses of mint tea. Carmody took a chair at one of the tables, positioning himself so he could look up along Rue Kaddour Bourkika; he had a clear angled view of the entrance to the courtyard. He ordered a glass of mint tea, closed his ears to the din around him, and waited.

He didn't have to wait long.

Inside of ten minutes Tobiere and Nicole Moreau came out through the passage, began to climb upward. Carmody dropped a couple of dinars on the table and glided after them. When they reached the upper plaza they crossed to where a dark green Citröen was parked at some distance from Carmody's Fiat. Carmody stayed hidden inside the Street of Many Steps until Nicole, who was driving the Citröen, circled past him; then he ran for the Fiat. There was only one street out of the plaza, so he had no trouble locating them and then following at a measured distance.

No trouble keeping the Citröen in sight, either, as they descended toward the harbor. The heavy traffic made speed impossible. The way Nicole drove told him she had no idea they were being tailed.

They proceeded past the Place des Martyrs to the harbor, turned west, and followed the shoreline crescent out of the city. Traffic thinned considerably then, and Nicole began driving at a hurry-up pace. Carmody dropped farther back, adjusting his speed to match hers.

The Citröen stayed on the coastal road for some thirty-five kilometers, until the village of Bou-Ismail took shape in the distance. Then the woman swung right toward the Mediterranean on a badly paved secondary road that slanted in among fields of vegetables. Carmody slowed, made the turn, fell back even farther. After another three kilometers, the Citröen swung off again and disappeared. Narrow sandy lane, Carmody saw when he reached the place, leading to an ancient farmhouse set at the foot of high, reddish dunes; the sea shimmered in the hot glow of the setting sun just beyond. The Citröen was drawn up near the farmhouse porch, Nicole and the man just emerging from it.

Carmody continued past the intersection by a hundred yards, to where a line of scruffy palms blocked out his vision of the farmhouse. Then he parked, got out into the humid, early-evening stillness.

There were no other cars in sight, no signs of life. He trotted across the road, climbed a fence into one of the fields, made his way toward the farmhouse. The vegetables were laid out in squared patches, separated by woven straw fences that acted as windbreaks. By moving in a low crouch, he was able to make good time without worrying about being spotted.

When he could see the farmhouse through chinks in the woven straw he stopped and gave it a long scan. Nothing moved over there, at least nothing outside. He worked his way in a wide loop, coming in from the rear, until a small barnlike outbuilding again cut off his view of the house. Then he ran across to a sagging wooden fence that enclosed the yard, climbed it, went to the wall of the barn and peered around the corner. Still no activity at the house.

He was sweating; he dried his face and cleared his eyes with the sleeve of his jacket. He drew the Beretta, ran in a low weave to the house's side wall, flattened back against it. Again he waited, listening. Quiet, except for the murmur of the sea beyond.

Carmody eased ahead to a closed window of dirt-streaked glass. As he leaned up close to it he could hear voices, but what they were saying to each other was unclear. A drawn shade kept him from seeing inside.

He went to the front corner, looked around it at the porch. Empty, the house door shut. He leaned back against the wall, the Beretta held down along his right leg, trying to make up his mind whether or not to break in on them. He didn't like the idea of that because he didn't know what the situation was in there. But he didn't like the idea of waiting around out here, either.

As it turned out, he didn't have to make a decision either way. The door opened abruptly and the blond man stepped out onto the porch. Carmody tensed. From inside he heard Nicole's sultry voice call out in French, "Hurry, *cherie*. It's getting late."

"We have plenty of time," the blond man answered. He turned to shut the door.

Carmody stepped around the corner, caught the porch rail, vaulted it. He landed running. The blond man spun toward him, confused, his hand fumbling at the pocket of his jacket. Carmody hit him in the face with the Beretta, a blow that sent him reeling, then veered to his left, kicked the door wide open, and went in low and fast with his gaze and the Beretta sweeping the room.

Nicole cried out, "*Zut alors merde!*" and a heavy gun crashed. She wasn't much of a shot; the bullet came nowhere near Carmody. He might have had to shoot her if she'd kept on potting at him but she didn't; she tried to run away through a rear doorway. There was a straight-backed chair on his immediate left, and he caught it up and threw it at her in one motion. She shrieked as it smacked into her backside, knocked her sideways against the door jamb; she went down hard to her knees. She still had the gun in her hand, a big Luger, but only for another couple of seconds. He was on her by then and he yanked it out of her hand before she could bring it to bear.

The fat sun-darkened man who had been sitting in one of the other chairs, and who had thrown himself to the floor when the shooting started, now yelled at Carmody from behind an ancient daybed, "Look out! The front door!"

Carmody's reaction was instantaneous: he whirled to his left, down and around into a shooter's crouch. The blond man stood in the doorway, the mate to Nicole's Luger in his hand, blood streaming down from a cut on his forehead. He fired once, wildly, just before Carmody shot him in the upper body. This time, when he fell back onto the porch, he stayed down and didn't move.

Carmody straightened slowly, letting breath out between his teeth, and looked over at Nicole. She was crouched against the wall, hating him with her eyes. He put her gun into one jacket pocket, went onto the porch and picked up the blond man's weapon and put that into the other jacket pocket.

The fat man came out from behind the daybed as Carmody walked back inside. His moonface was slick with sweat. He said, "He's dead? You killed him?"

"No. He'll ve if he gets medical attention."

That disappointed the fat man. With good reason, Carmody thought. There were marks on his face, arms, neck: beaten on and burned with cigarettes, among other indignities. Carmody watched him turn blazing eyes on the woman, call her a vicious name in French, take a step toward her with his hands clenched. He stopped him halfway by catching hold of his shoulder.

"She's not worth the trouble. Leave her alone."

The fat man took a shuddering breath, relaxed a little. His pained eyes focused on Carmody without recognition. "Who are you?"

"Carmody."

"*Mon Dieu!* But how—?"

"We'll get to that. You're Tobiere, right? The *real* Paul Tobiere?"

Convulsive nod. "They were going to kill me. Nicole and that . . . that *fils de putain.*"

"I figured as much. Who is he—the blond?"

"His name is Chagal," Tobiere said. "One of Nicole's filthy lovers."

Carmody said, "They were trying to pass him off as you, to take advantage of your arrangement with me." He didn't add that they must have known of his particular code of ethics, that he couldn't be bought off and that any kind of double-dealing was anathema to him. One hint that the real Tobiere had been robbed and murdered and he'd have called off the deal immediately.

"I was a fool to trust her," Tobiere said. "But I believed she cared for me; I believed—"

"*Cochon! Je t'emmerge, à pied, à cheval et en voiture!*"

Carmody said, "Shut up, Nicole." His tone said he didn't want any arguments. She didn't give him any.

"How did you know to come here?" the fat man asked.

Carmody told him how he'd followed Nicole and Chagal from the Casbah.

"But what made you suspect Chagal was not me?"

"Several things. She seemed to be running the show, not him; that didn't jibe with what Achmed told me. Neither did the way he acted. Achmed said you were frightened and anxious after what happened to you en route from the Sudan. Chagal wasn't either one. Then there was the fact that you lived in the Sudan for years, came here through the Libyan Desert. No man can spend time in that kind of desert country without picking up a black tan like you have, or at least some sun color. Chagal is pale—no tan, no burn. He's been nowhere near Sudan or the Libyan Desert. Not long out of France, probably."

Tobiere nodded. "I owe you my life, *m'sieu.*"

"I'll settle for ten percent of those gems," Carmody said. "Where are they? You didn't tell Nicole and Chagal or you'd

be dead already."

"No, but I . . . I think I would have." He shuddered. "The things they did to me . . . the things they threatened to do . . ."

"Never mind that. The gems, Tobiere. Are they here?"

"Nearby. Shall I get them?"

"We'll both go get them. If they're as advertised, you'll be on a boat for France by midnight."

"Nicole? You will kill her before we leave here?"

"I'm not an assassin," Carmody said.

"But they were going to kill me . . ."

"They've got each other, her and Chagal, and they've got Algiers. That's worse than being dead. That's a living hell."

He took Tobiere's arm and prodded him out into the breathless North African twilight.

DEATH WARRANT

The house was on Görtnerstrasse, in one of Vienna's older residential neighborhoods. Stark beech and linden trees, like gray bones stripped of flesh by the winter wind, lined the dark street on both sides; a huge willow grew in the yard fronting the house, just beyond the gate affixed with the numerals 629. The house itself was small, peak-roofed, with a wood-studded facade.

Carmody pushed open the gate, went up and used the knocker on the front door. He stood with his shoulders hunched inside the heavy wool topcoat he wore. In his right hand he carried an oversized attache case; his Beretta was in its usual place, in the belt half-holster at his side.

He had been in Vienna for less than four hours, expected to remain here only until tomorrow morning. He had other business elsewhere. Vienna may have been a city of intrigue once, in its postwar occupation days, but not any more. It had long since reverted to its bland, traditional stance as a citadel of history, music and the arts. It was no place, these days, for a man in Carmody's line of work. He would have starved if he'd tried to do business here on a regular basis.

There were footsteps inside and the door opened to reveal a smiling, well-dressed man of about fifty. Sharp blue eyes, brushed blond hair, squared chin with a cleft: Anton Varndal. Bruckner had described him in detail.

"Herr Carmody?"

"That's right. And you're Varndal."

"I am, yes." Varndal seized his hand, pumped it rapidly several times. The Austrians loved to shake hands, and they did it with plenty of vigor, as if they were working the handle of a fitness machine.

"Invite me in," Carmody said. "It's damned cold out here."

"But of course, *herr.*"

Inside, Carmody unbuttoned both his topcoat and his suit jacket so he would have easy access to the Beretta if he needed it; he was a cautious man. Varndal led him into a parlor filled with heavy old furniture. The room had a faint musty smell, as if it had been closed up for some time.

Varndal asked, "Have you brought the transmitter?"

"I wouldn't be here if I hadn't."

"Please, you will show it to me."

"You still owe me eight thousand dollars, U.S. currency."

"But of course. May I examine the transmitter first?"

"Be my guest."

Carmody handed him the attache case. Varndal, eyes bright with expectancy, took it to a table and opened it. Carefully he lifted out its contents.

The radio transmitter was small, portable, battery-operated. It was also delicately constructed to put out a certain signal of ultra-high frequency and strength, with a variation of no more than a plus or minus .03. A transmitter of that type was not easy to obtain, particularly if you didn't want its origin traced because you had a use for it that was at best extralegal. That was why Varndal had come to Carmody through his Austrian contact, Josef Bruckner. Carmody had connections in every country in

Europe and most of those in the free world; he could supply just about anything if the price was right.

Varndal had wanted the transmitter by today's date. Carmody had no real interest in why the Austrian wanted it; his only interest was in the ten thousand dollars Varndal had agreed to pay—two thousand faith money in advance, the balance on delivery. He minded his business, his clients minded theirs. Complete discretion was one of the commodities he had to sell.

"Satisfied, Varndal?"

"Quite satisfied, *herr*. This is of excellent quality."

"Did you expect any different?"

"No, no. I expected just what you have delivered."

"Then you can pay me now."

"*Natürlich,* Herr Carmody." He put the transmitter back into the case, left the case on the table. "You will come with me to my study, please?"

"If that's where the money is."

Varndal nodded, smiled, and moved out of the parlor and down a hallway to a closed door at the rear. He opened the door, took a step into the darkened room beyond. There was a snicking sound as he touched a wall switch; light flooded the room. Carmody, following close behind the Austrian, saw that it was a study, all right, but one in which most of the furnishings were covered by heavy dust cloths. He pulled up short, reaching for the Beretta.

Varndal was already turning, one hand upraised, something long and thin in it that he'd had concealed under his suit coat. Carmody tried to duck and draw the Beretta at the same time—but he wasn't quite fast enough. The something in Varndal's hand collided with his head just above the left ear.

Blinding pain.

Legs jellying, the floor coming up to meet him.

Humming in his ears like a high-speed drill.

Door slamming, far away.

Black.

Carmody came out of it, rolled over, sat up with his head hanging between his knees. The butt of the Beretta, still holstered, dug into his side. Nausea roiled in his stomach. The pain in his head was savage—two jagged lines of it, like parallel lightning arcs, that seemed to run upward from his neck to the top of his skull. His thoughts were muddled. Concussion?

Gingerly he touched the place where Varndal had hit him, found a pulpy area beneath the mat of hair that grew thickly over his ears; the hair had cushioned the blow. There was no blood. He got onto his knees, then onto his feet. Leaned against the wall until the nausea eased and his thinking straightened out. Then he looked at his wristwatch. Eight-twenty. He had been unconscious a little less than an hour.

The lines of pain glowed hotly as he went out of the study and down the hallway, pulling open other doors, looking inside rooms. All the rooms had dustcovers like shrouds over the furniture. Upstairs it was the same: dustcovers and must. The house *had* been closed up for a long time.

There was no sign of Varndal.

Carmody went back downstairs and outside, leaving the front door standing wide open. The winter wind seemed colder, sharper. He got into the rented Mercedes and burned rubber pulling away from the curb, his body hunched, his big hands in a stranglehold on the steering wheel.

It took him the better part of half an hour to get to Grinzing. The village had an old-world atmosphere and was well known for its wine inns and wine festivals; the combination attracted the tourists in droves in the autumn months. This time of year the locals were the inns' best customers.

Carmody parked in front of a grape-arbored *Weinstube* called Die Moselle, after one of the local whites, and entered. Most of the high-backed wooden booths were filled—women in dirndals, men in *lederhosen*, people in more modern dress. Two heavyset men in gypsy costume were playing a spirited *zigeuner* tune on an accordion and a violin. Carmody barely heard the music; his attention was on the crowd, scanning faces. The pain in his head had dulled to a bearable throbbing. The heat in him now was all rage.

Bruckner was sitting with a blonde who looked as if she could and often did eat an entire *Sachertorte mit Schlag* at one sitting: she must have weighed about two-twenty. They were in a corner booth at the rear, drinking wine and toasting each other with their glasses and their eyes. Carmody leaned close to Bruckner and said, "Get rid of the woman. We need to talk."

Bruckner, thin and bony, with wildly unruly hair and a thick mustache, said in bewildered tones, "Something is the matter, Herr Carmody?"

"Damn right. Get rid of her, Bruckner."

Bruckner nodded, patted the blonde's thick arm and said something to her in German that Carmody didn't understand. The woman gave Carmody a hostile look, got ponderously out of the booth, waddled away.

Carmody sat down. "Your boy Varndal tried to crack my skull," he said. "Knocked me out and made off with the transmitter. I don't like to be double-crossed, Bruckner. I don't like it one bit."

Bruckner looked shocked. "But . . . but why? Why would he do such a foolish thing?"

"You tell me."

"But I have no idea . . ."

"You said he was all right."

"It seemed so to me, Herr Carmody. With him I spoke three times before I agreed to call you. He said nothing to give suspicion . . ."

"Didn't you check him out, for Christ's sake?"

"As well as I could. *Bitte, herr,* I—"

"What did he want the transmitter for?"

"He didn't tell me. And since it isn't required that you—"

"Where does he live?"

"The house where you met him—?"

"Vacant," Carmody said. "Nobody lives there now. Dustcovers over most of the furniture, except in the parlor downstairs."

"But if Varndal was there, if he had keys, the owners he must know . . ."

"That's right. And one of us is going to find out who they are. Fast, Bruckner. Tonight."

"*Jawöhl*, Herr Carmody."

"How did you get in touch with Varndal? By telephone, public meeting place, what?"

"With Anya Berg I left messages," Bruckner said. "Varndal and I met here, always."

"Who would Anya Berg be?"

"The proprietress of a shop near the canal."

"What kind of shop?"

"A tobacco shop. Also she sells information."

"Yes? And where does she fit into this?"

"It was Anya who gave Varndal my name. And yours."

"Does she know Varndal personally?"

Bruckner shook his head. "*Ich weiss nicht*. She said he had been referred by a friend."

"What friend?"

"I saw no reason to ask her," Bruckner said defensively. "She is an old friend—"

"You've got shit for brains, you know that?"

"Herr Carmody, I—"

"You know where Anya Berg lives? How to get in touch with her at this time of night?"

"Yes."

"Go call her then. Will she answer the phone herself if she's home?"

"Yes. She lives alone."

"If she answers, don't say anything to her. Just hang up. All I want to know is if she's home."

Bruckner left the booth. Carmody lit a thin, black cigar as he waited. There was a strong dose of urgency in his anger: he had to find Anton Varndal quickly. If he didn't, word would leak out about the doublecross—and others would try the same thing in the future. He couldn't operate if there was even a hint that he was vulnerable.

Bruckner was back inside of five minutes, mopping sweat from his forehead with a silk handkerchief. "She is home," he said.

"What's her address?"

Bruckner told him. "What will you do when you see her?"

"Ask her some questions."

"She is not responsible for Varndal—"

"Let's hope not," Carmody said. "As for you, get to work checking into that house on Görtnerstrasse. Then go to your apartment and wait for me to contact you. Clear?"

"*Klar*, Herr Carmody."

Outside in the Mercedes, Carmody consulted his city map of Vienna. Anya Berg lived off the Ringstrasse, the boulevard that circled the old Inner City—easy enough to find. He left the map open on the seat beside him, put the car in gear.

Carmody said, "Anya Berg?"

The woman standing in the doorway was in her thirties, brown-haired, attractive in an overripe way. Her brown eyes were shrewd, calculating. "Yes?"

"I'm Carmody. Shall we talk inside?"

Anya Berg studied him for a few seconds, shrugged, led him into a small sitting room. "Why are you interested in me, Herr Carmody?"

"Bruckner tells me you sent Anton Varndal to him."

"I did that, yes. Why?"

"I'm looking for Varndal. Where does he live?"

"I have no idea."

"You don't know him personally?"

"Not well, no. He was sent to me by a mutual friend."

"So Bruckner tells me. What's this friend's name?"

"Perhaps I shouldn't tell you that—"

"You'd better tell me. I'm in no mood for games, lady.

What's the friend's name?"

"Dietrich. Viktor Dietrich."

"What's his connection with Varndal?"

"Viktor once handled a transaction for him."

"What kind of transaction?"

"The sale of some small property."

"Yes? Dietrich's a real estate agent?"

"Among other interests."

"I'll bet. Where do I find him?"

"You intend him no harm? He is a good friend—"

"He won't get hurt if he's cooperative."

Anya Berg hesitated, but not for long. The look in Carmody's flat eyes convinced her to be candid. She said, "Burgplatz, in Volksprater. Number ninety-seven."

Carmody said, "Don't call him after I leave. I wouldn't like it if I have trouble finding him. Neither would he and neither would you."

"I will not call him," she said.

A sleek black sedan was just pulling into Viktor Dietrich's driveway when Carmody rolled past. He parked four doors down from the Swiss-style house, ran across the street into the shadows cast by a willow that grew on a neighboring lawn. The wind off the Danube was like ice against his skin. In the distance, the bell in the Cathedral of Saint Stephen tolled the hour: eleven o'clock.

Carmody climbed over a small boundary fence, the Beretta in his hand. His head had begun to ache malignantly again. He eased across a strip of lawn, into the darkness of Dietrich's garage.

The man who stood there at the open car door said in startled tones, "*Wer ist da?*"

"Viktor Dietrich?"

"*Ja. Was ist Ihnen denn?*"

"Don't close the door. Just stand where you are."

Carmody moved ahead to where he had a clearer look at the man: tall, paunchy, sixtyish. There was no one else in the car or in the garage. He said then, "I'm looking for

Anton Varndal. I understand you're a friend of his."

"Yes, I know him," Dietrich said, in English now. "Who are you?"

"Never mind that," Carmody said. "I've got business with Varndal and I can't seem to find him. Maybe you can tell me where to look."

"You have tried his home?"

"I don't know the address. What is it?"

". . . What sort of business do you have with him?"

"My business, not yours. Tell me where he lives."

"Not before you tell me who you are and what you—"

Carmody moved forward again, let Dietrich see the Beretta. "Who I am isn't important to you. This is."

Dietrich went rigid. There was fear in his voice when he said, "What do you want with me? What are you going to do?"

"If you answer my questions, nothing. Just be cooperative—that's all you have to do."

"I . . . I will do whatever you say."

"Smart man. When did you last see Varndal?"

"Last evening. At nine o'clock."

"Where?"

"Here, my home. He came to see me."

"Why?"

"To ask me for a favor."

"What kind of favor? Loan him the keys to a vacant house, maybe?"

Surprise made Dietrich blink. "How did you know that?"

"I'm the reason he wanted the vacant house," Carmody said thinly. "I don't suppose Varndal told you the reason for this favor."

"No, he told me nothing."

"Why did you let him have the keys?"

"I . . . we are friends."

"Sure you are," Carmody said. "How much did he pay you?"

Dietrich hesitated, looked at the gun in Carmody's

hand, and said, "Two thousand schillings."

"All right. Now let's talk about Anya Berg."

"Anya? You know her?"

"We've met. You sent Varndal to her. Why?"

"No," Dietrich said, "I did not send him to her. I gave her name to Varndal, yes, but that is all. He went to her, used my name without permission."

"She told you that?"

"Yes. Afterward."

"I'll bet you were upset," Carmody said. "You and Anya are old friends too, I suppose. Everybody's an old friend of everybody else in Vienna."

"We have known each other many years."

"She tell you Varndal was after a radio transmitter?"

"Radio transmitter? No."

"He didn't mention it either?"

"No."

"Any idea why he'd want one with a special frequency?"

"No, I have no idea."

"You'd better not be lying to me, Dietrich."

"Why should I lie? I have no wish to be shot."

"Just keep thinking that way. Where does Varndal live?"

"On Kurzgasse, near the Prater Platz. Number twenty."

"Private house?"

"Yes. The neighborhood is mixed."

"Mixed?"

"Business establishments and private homes."

"If Varndal isn't there, where do I look for him?"

"I don't know," Dietrich said.

"No? I thought you were such good friends."

"Not so very good. No."

"So you don't know any of his other friends? Or where he hangs out?"

"No. We have drinks a few times, we have some little business together, that is all."

"Like I said, Dietrich, you'd better not be lying to me. If I find out you are, I'll be back."

Carmody backed away, and as he glided out of the

garage he could hear Dietrich breathing noisily in the darkness. He jumped the boundary fence, crossed under the willows, and slid into the Mercedes again.

Kurzgasse and the Prater Platz were in the old Russian-occupied sector, not too far from the Prater, Vienna's big public park. It was an old, rundown neighborhood, not quite a slum but sliding in that direction. Plain trees lined Kurzgasse, their bare branches moving in the wind like crone's fingers.

Number twenty was a one-story brick house, nondescript and lightless. Carmody rang the bell four times; chimes echoed emptily within each time. He went to work on the flimsy lock, had it open in less than a minute. He stepped inside, shut the door behind him, took the pencil flashlight from the pocket of his topcoat.

He followed the beam through five rooms, opening drawers and closets and cabinets. The search told him Varndal had moved out, and in something of a hurry: important belongings gone, not so important ones left behind. Carmody wondered if he were following an ice-cold trail; Varndal had had more than enough time to make plane or train connections out of Vienna. But it was just as likely that the purpose Varndal had for the transmitter was here in the city or its environs. If that was the case, he intended to use it tonight or early tomorrow. Otherwise, why had he wanted it by today's date? And why had he already made preparations to skip?

A door at one end of the kitchen caught Carmody's eye. When he opened it, the flash revealed a set of stairs leading downward. He felt along the inside wall, found a light switch, flicked it on. Below was a cellar, small, cramped, smelling of dampness and mold . . . and something sour he couldn't identify. He went down the stairs, sweeping the torch beam from side to side.

The floor was earthen, muddy, trenched along the bases of the stone walls from water seepage and erosion caused by heavy winter rains. Carmody prowled among stacks of miscellaneous cartons, examined tools and bottles and jars on a narrow workbench. None of it told him anything useful. He took a few steps toward the rear wall, and the odd sour odor seemed stronger over there. The hair on the back of his scalp prickled. He drew a deep, slow breath. Now he knew what the smell was.

He moved ahead, shone his flash along the muddied depressions at the base of the wall. The light picked up something. He walked closer, bent at the waist.

The something was a human foot encased in a heavy black shoe.

Carmody went to the workbench, took up the hand trowel he'd seen there, carried it to where the foot poked up out of the mud. He knelt on a bundle of newspapers and began digging. It didn't take him long to uncover the corpse. The flesh had started to decompose, but the size and the clothing and what was left of the features told him it had once been a heavyset, middle-aged man.

The odor was bad now; it made his stomach queasy again, renewed the throbbing in his head. Quickly he searched the body, came up with a sodden, decaying wallet. Most of the papers inside were unreadable, but some of the cards were protected by celluloid wrappers. He could see that one was an identification card, another a union card; and he knew enough German to translate the information contained on them.

The dead man's name had been Karl Heinz. His occupation: electrician. And his business address was listed as 22 Kurzgasse, the building next door to this house.

Carmody stood up. Things were beginning to make some sense now. But not enough, not yet, to lead him to Varndal.

He climbed the cellar steps, left the house by the rear door. Several stunted fir trees grew in the back yard, their crowns partially obscured by a gathering winter mist. Beyond the farthest of them, a mesh fence topped with barbed wire separated Varndal's property from the cluttered rear grounds of Karl Heinz's electrical shop. Despite the barbed wire, the fence looked scaleable.

It was. Carmody used his gloved hands to bunch and depress the strands of wire so he could get his legs over, then dropped down on the far side. As soon as his feet touched the asphalt, he was moving through the misty dark to the rear door.

The lock here was just as flimsy as the one on Varndal's front entrance. He picked it quickly, drifted inside. He put the pencil flash on long enough to determine that this was the workshop and that two closed doors led off of it. The one in the facing wall would open on the customer entrance, he thought; the one in the right-hand wall probably led to an office of some kind.

It was the office he wanted, so he crossed to that door and tried the knob. It turned under his fingers. The room beyond was small, too neat, as if it had been straightened recently—probably by relatives of Karl Heinz in the days since the electrician's disappearance. Three sets of file cabinets huddled opposite a functional metal desk. Apparently Heinz had done a brisk business.

Carmody put the light on the cabinets. The files were arranged according to date rather than in alphabetical order, which made the hunting easier. He found the most recent file, dated the previous month, and went through the papers methodically. There was nothing for him among them.

On the desk were two wire baskets filled with papers. He looked through one, found nothing, and started on the second. A three-page invoice, with a typed letter signed by someone named Gunter Amerling stapled to it, caught his attention. The first paragraph of the letter, under a printed letterhead, said in German that Amerling was enclosing a check in payment of the invoice.

Carmody deciphered the rest of the letter, glanced through the invoice. This was what he'd been looking for—the key to Varndal's scheme and Varndal's where-abouts. The letter and check must have come in *after* Heinz's murder; Varndal hadn't known about them or he'd have destroyed them as he had the other records dealing with the Amerling job.

Carmody looked at his watch. Half past twelve. If he was right about Varndal using the transmitter tonight, there might still be enough time to get to him before he was finished. Varndal wouldn't risk doing the job too early.

He went out the front way. In the Mercedes again, he checked the city map. The address on Amerling's letterhead was a short, twisty road on the outskirts of the city, to the northwest. He judged it to be about a thirty-minute drive from Kurzgasse.

As he drove, his foot heavy on the accelerator, he thought the whole thing through. The job Karl Heinz had done for Gunter Amerling was the installation of a new, "burglar proof" safe—the type that had no combination dial, that was in fact a plain steel box without any external locking device. It operated by means of a crystal-controlled radio transmitter of ultra-high frequency which activated a locking device built into the door. If somebody tried to open it with a variable-frequency transmitter, or tried to blow it or torch it open, alarms would be set off inside the house and at the local police station. It was all very modern and theoretically foolproof —except that it didn't take into account the unforeseen factor.

Anton Varndal was that unforeseen factor.

Living next door to Heinz's electrical shop, perhaps a drinking companion or casual friend of Heinz's, Varndal had somehow found out about the Amerling job; and with that knowledge he'd devised his scheme to steal whatever it was that Amerling kept inside the safe. The plan was simple. Acquire a small, portable transmitter of the same frequency and strength as the unit which operated Amerling's safe, one that put out a signal with a variation of no more than a plus or minus .03 so as not to set off the alarms. Then keep tabs on Amerling's movements, and on a night when he would be away from home, break into his house and loot the safe.

Varndal must have approached Heinz with his plan—

probably offered him a fee or a split to manufacture the second transmitter. But Heinz had balked, threatened to go to the police or to Gunter Amerling. So Varndal had killed him to keep him quiet. Burying the body in his own cellar served two purposes: he didn't have to risk moving it far, and it wasn't likely to be found anytime soon. Who would suspect Heinz's next-door neighbor of murdering him?

Then Varndal had found out from Dietrich about Anya Berg, and from her about Josef Bruckner and Carmody. He must have had to scratch to come up with the two-thousand-dollar down payment — and he'd been unable to scratch up the eight-thousand-dollar balance. That and the big score at Amerling's had made him desperate enough to risk clubbing Carmody at the Görtnerstrasse house tonight. And that had been his first big mistake.

His second was leaving Carmody alive.

His second had signed his own death warrant.

The area in which Gunter Amerling lived was in the foothills of the Eastern Alps, just below the Weinerwald. High-walled estates had been built at staggered intervals along the narrow, twisting lane. Higher up, over the crests of the hills, the thick stands of pine that formed the Vienna Woods were hidden behind a floating wall of mist. At this level, birch and beech trees, branches winter-stripped, rose in ghostly clusters.

Carmody found the number he wanted on one of two stone pillars that supported an iron-filligree gate. Through the gate he could just make out the estate road before it vanished among more trees; the house was invisible from here. He drove past the gate several hundred yards, left the car in close to the stone wall that enclosed the Amerling estate. The wall was high and smooth-sided, but by standing on the roof of the Mercedes he was able to hoist himself atop it. He dropped down on the other side, stood for a moment to reconnoiter. Nightlights glowed faintly through the mist, at an angle to his left. He moved that way, through more of the ghost-white birch.

When he came out of the trees he could see the house a hundred yards away—imposing, gabled, made of or faced with stone. It was shrouded in mist, dark except for the nightlights that illuminated the front drive and part of the estate road. Off to the left of the road, set back into the trees, was what looked to be a caretaker's cottage. A light burned in the cottage's front window, dimly. Everything seemed quiet, normal.

Keeping to heavy shadows, Carmody went toward the house at an angle until he reached the side wall. He moved along there to the rear. The windows on both levels were shuttered on that side, the shutters securely locked.

He crossed through a side garden, onto a stone-floored patio. A set of French doors opening off the patio were locked. Carmody drifted around to the far side of the house, found a high, short wing—the servants' or kitchen entrance. All dark over there too. Either there weren't any live-in servants or they were already in bed asleep.

Carmody eased beyond the wing, along the side wall toward the front. He was halfway there when something short and worm-thin skittered toward him across the ground, undulating in the chill wind. He bent, caught it, held it up to his eyes. A length of black wire, a foot long, cut out of an electrical line. Varndal's work, he thought. It figured that there would be some kind of standard alarm system on the doors and windows, and that Varndal knew the location of the wiring from Heinz's records—knew the right place to make a cut to disable the system.

Been here and gone? Or still here?

Carmody's lips were slash-thin, drawn in hard against his teeth. He started forward again. The shutters on the window ahead of him slapped softly against the stone siding of the house: they had been opened and refastened from within, but not securely. He edged up to the window. Through the gap in the shutters he saw darkness—and then a flicker of light. The light went out, flickered again: flashlight beam.

Question answered: Varndal was still here.

Carmody backed away to the wing, crouched in the shadows with the Beretta tight-gripped in his fingers. The wind blew icy fog against his cheeks, swirled leaves and twigs around his feet. He barely noticed. His eyes were intent on the window.

It was ten minutes before the shutters spread wide and the dark, cloth-capped figure emerged from inside. In one hand was an obviously heavy satchel; in the other, a blob that would be the portable radio transmitter. Varndal set both of these on the ground, reached up to close the shutters again. Then he looked both ways along the house, picked up the satchel and transmitter, started into the woods that grew close on this side.

Carmody followed, moving laterally in the shadows at first to get himself behind Varndal; then he matched the Austrian's pace, close enough to keep him in sight through the trees and mist. Varndal went at a labored trot, slowed by the combined weight of the satchel and the transmitter. He didn't look back. He didn't think there was any reason to look back.

The stone wall materialized ahead. Varndal struggled on at a faster pace. He was panting audibly when he reached the base of the wall. He put the satchel and transmitter down again, leaned against the stones to catch his breath. Carmody kept moving, the wind and the carpeting of leaves underfoot masking his approach.

Varndal didn't hear him until Carmody was less than ten yards away. He spun from the wall, crouching, his hand tugging at something in his belt. The something jerked free, raised in Varndal's grasp, and Carmody shot him twice with the Beretta. Varndal yelled, gasped, sagged to his knees. The gun he'd drawn came loose and made a dull, plopping sound in the leaves.

Carmody ran up to him, ready to fire again, but there was no fight left in the Austrian. He stared at Carmody, his eyes shiny with pain and recognition, with disbelief. His lips worked, tried to form words. Then he flopped forward, his cap falling off. He didn't move, would never move again.

Carmody put the Beretta away, caught up the heavy satchel and the transmitter, walked along the wall to the gate. He didn't hurry because there was no longer any need to hurry. If the caretaker had heard the shots and came to investigate, it would take him quite a while to locate Varndal's body in the dark and then to sound an alarm.

At the gate, Carmody shoved the satchel and transmitter through the iron bars. Climbing the gate was no easy task—the bars were spike-pointed at the top—but there were no cars on the road and he took his time. He got over without doing himself any damage.

The satchel and transmitter went into the Mercedes' trunk. He started the engine, made a U-turn, drove back past the gate without lights and without seeing anybody on the grounds inside. Ten minutes later he was on a main Vienna artery, on his way to Grinzing and Josef Bruckner's apartment.

Bruckner said, "Gold coins! So that is what Varndal stole from Amerling's safe."

Carmody nodded. Commemorative European gold coins, to be exact—over a hundred of them. That was why the satchel had been so heavy, Amerling was a coin collector, one of the breed that specialized in the rare and fancy gold variety.

"What a fine price these will bring on the black market!" Bruckner said. "Perhaps as much as three hundred thousand dollars, *nein?*"

"*Nein,*" Carmody said. "They won't bring a cent because they're not going out on the market."

"But . . . I do not understand . . ."

"The coins go back to Amerling in the morning, in a package you're going to make up and mail. There were thirty thousand schillings in the safe, too, that Varndal took with him. It doesn't amount to the eight thousand dollars he owed me for the transmitter but it's close enough.

That's all I want out of the deal."

Bruckner looked stricken. "I still do not understand, Herr Carmody. Three hundred thousand American dollars . . ."

"Wouldn't make any difference if the value was one million or ten million," Carmody said. "I'm not a thief. I play games with the law, I break the law for money, but I'm not a common thief."

He left the coins with Bruckner and drove to his hotel on Mariahilferstrasse. Bruckner would do as he'd been told; he had no desire to wind up like Anton Varndal. And it would be the last thing he'd ever do for Carmody. In the morning, after Carmody salved his aching head with some sleep, he would arrange to delay his departure from Vienna by twenty-four hours. Then he would make some phone calls, get some names, conduct an interview or two, and pick somebody who wasn't a fool to be his new Austrian contact.

One mistake was all you got when you worked for Carmody.

One mistake in his business was one too many.

BLOOD MONEY

Carmody spent the morning at Bacino di Borechi, checking out the boat and captain Della Robbia had hired for the run south to Sardinia. The boat was forty-two feet and twenty years old—the *Piraeus,* flying a Greek flag. She was scabrous and salt-scarred, her fittings flecked with rust, but she seemed seaworthy and she had an immaculate power-plant: a twin-screw GMC diesel, well-tuned and shiny clean.

The captain looked all right too. He was an Australian named Vickers, who had been in Venice for a couple of years and who had handled some other smuggling jobs for Della Robbia, one involving a boatload of illegal aliens from Albania. Della Robbia said he was the best man available and he probably was. Sardinia would be a piece of cake compared to getting into Albanian waters and then out again safely with forty-three passengers.

From the *bacino* Carmody took a water taxi to St. Mark's Square. Della Robbia hadn't shown up yet at the open-air cafe on the Piazzeta. Carmody took a table, ordered a cup of cappucino. It was a warm, windy

September day, and the square was jammed with tourists, vendors, free-lance artists, the ever-present pigeons. On the wide fronting basin, into which emptied Venice's two major canals, the Grand and the Giudecca, gondolas and water taxis, passenger ferries and small commercial craft maneuvered in bright confusion. The sun turned the placid water a glinting silver, gave it a mercurial aspect.

Cities were just cities to Carmody—places to be and to work in and to leave again—but Venice intruded on his consciousness more than most. For one thing, you didn't have to worry about traffic problems because it had no automobiles. It was built on a hundred little islands inter-connected by a hundred and fifty bridges, and you got from place to place on foot through narrow, winding interior streets or by water taxi and ferry. The pocked, sagging look of most of the ancient buildings was due to the fact that the city was sinking at the rate of five inches per century; the look and smell of the four hundred canals was the result of pollution. It was a seedy, charming, ugly, beautiful, dangerous, amiable city—one Carmody under-stood, and felt at ease in, and worked well in.

He had been sitting there for fifteen minutes when Della Robbia came hurrying between the two red granite obelisks that marked the beginning of the Piazzeta. Dark, craggy-featured, in his middle thirties, wearing a light gray suit and a pair of fat sunglasses, Della Robbia looked exactly like what he was: a minor Italian gangster. That worked in his favor more often than not. Because he looked like a thug, a lot of people figured he wasn't one.

When Della Robbia sat down Carmody said, "You make the arrangements for the launch?"

"Just as you instructed, Signor Carmody."

"What did you tell the driver?"

"Only that he is to pick up a passenger, transport him to an address he will be given, pick up additional passengers, and then proceed to a boat in the Lagoon."

"Does he speak English?"

"Enough to understand simple directions."

"You're sure he can be trusted?"

"*Assolutamente, signor.*"

"He'll be ready to go tonight?"

"Any time you wish."

"The way it looks now," Carmody said, "we can do it tonight. I went to see Vickers and his boat this morning. I'm satisfied."

"I was certain you would be."

Carmody lit one of his thin, black cigars. "I'll call you later and let you know what time the launch driver is to pick me up. Where do I meet him?"

"The Rio de Fontego, at the foot of Via Giordano," Della Robbia said. "A quiet place without much water traffic, so you can be sure you are not followed."

"How far is the Rio de Fontego from my hotel?"

"Ten minutes by water taxi."

"All right, good."

"There are other arrangements to be made?"

"No. I'll handle the rest of it. But stay where I can reach you the rest of the day."

Della Robbia said, "*Va bene,*" and got to his feet. "A safe journey, Signor Carmody." He lifted his hand in a salute and moved off across the Piazzeta, disappeared into the crowd of tourists and pigeons in front of the Ducal Palace.

Carmody finished his cigar, walked away from St. Marks along the Grand Canal quay. He found a stop for water taxis, rode in one to the Rio de Fontego. It turned out to be near the arched Rialto Bridge, in the approximate center of the city. Via Giordano was a quiet street lined with old houses and a few small shops that would be shuttered after dark. From the seawall at the foot of the street he could see for some distance both ways along the canal and back along Via Giordano. Della Robbia had chosen well. Carmody hadn't expected otherwise, but he hadn't had any prior dealings with the Italian and he was a careful man besides.

He got back into the water taxi and went to keep his

appointment with Renzo Lucarelli.

Lucarelli was forty-two years old, thick-necked and wolf-eyed. Until recently he'd sported a luxuriant black military mustache that made him look more like an Italian Army colonel than a criminal on the run. Carmody had had him shave it off for his new identity and passport photo. Lucarelli missed the mustache; he kept fingering his upper lip self-consciously, as if he felt conspicuous without it.

He peered at the map spread open on the table, laid a thick forefinger on an X marked on the Venice Lagoon. "This boat, this *Piraeus*, will meet the launch here?" he asked.

Carmody said, "That's right."

"But we can be seen from the Quartiere."

"Who's going to see us?"

"Gambresca has many eyes. So does the *carabinieri—*"

"Gambresca can't have any idea when or how you're leaving Venice; neither can the government. And there's nothing along the Quartiere except warehouses and anchored freighters. Even if we're seen, nobody's going to question the transfer. Launches take passengers out to private vessels all the time. I know, I checked it."

"But a little farther out on the Lagoon . . ."

"Listen," Carmody said, "we want to stay in the shipping roads. Any farther out and we're inviting the attention you're so worried about. Besides, the quicker we get onto the *Piraeus* and out of the Lagoon, the better."

Lucarelli stroked his barren upper lip. "You are certain of this man Vickers?"

"Della Robbia vouches for him. And I'll be along to see that he's no problem."

"I do not like putting my life in the hands of men I have never met."

"Yes? You've only known me four days."

"I have known of your great reputation for many years," Lucarelli said, and fingered his naked lip again. "The

Piraeus is old and rusty, you said. Suppose something happens to her engines before we reach Sardinia? She might even sink in a sudden squall—"

"For Christ's sake, Lucarelli, I told you the boat was all right. Don't you think I know what I'm doing? How do you figure I got that reputation of mine? Now stop fussing like an old woman and quit asking questions I've already answered."

Lucarelli gestured apologetically. "It is only that I am nervous, Signor Carmody. I meant no offense." He lifted the glass at his elbow, drank off the last of the red wine it contained. Then he glanced over to where his woman sat paging through a magazine. "Rita, another glass of wine."

She stood immediately, came to the table. She was tall and plump and huge-breasted, with thick black hair pulled back tight from her forehead and fastened with a jeweled barette; Carmody thought she's have made a fine Rueben's nude. He preferred slender, less top-heavy women himself. Her expression was neutral but her eyes betrayed her unease. She was not bearing up under the waiting any better than Lucarelli.

Lucarelli gave her his glass, then said to Carmody, "You will have some wine now, Signor Carmody?"

"No. And you'd better go easy on that stuff yourself. If we go tonight I don't want you drunk or anywhere near it."

"Then it *will* be tonight?"

"Everything's set for it. I don't see any reason for holding off another day."

"Good. Ah, good."

Rita poured Lucarelli's glass full of Chianti, brought it back to him, went over and sat down again with her magazine. She hadn't said a word since Carmody's arrival twenty minutes ago.

The room they were in was the main parlor of a crumbling building perched on the edge of Rio San Spirito, in a northeastern sector not far from Laguna Morta and the island that served as the city cemetery. A poor neighborhood; and a poor house that had waterstained wallpaper, rococo lighting fixtures tarnished by age, and a lingering odor of damp decay mixed with the fish-and-garbage reek of the canal outside. It was a long way from the walled palace-house Lucarelli claimed to have occupied on Lido Island before the fat little world he'd created for himself had collapsed.

Lucarelli was, or had been, a smuggler and black-marketeer who dealt in the lucrative commodity of cigarettes. The Italian government owned a monopoly on the manufacture and sale of all tobacco products, and imposed a high duty on the import of American and English brands. Since most Italians preferred the imported to the raw homemade variety, and the demand grew greater every year, tons of contraband cigarettes were smuggled annually into the country. Lucarelli's operation, independent of syndicate ties, had been one of the largest in the northern provinces. He'd had cigarettes coming into Venice across the gulf from Trieste and down from Switzerland, and a fleet of trucks and men to distribute them throughout Italy.

But then the Guardia de Finanza, the agents of the ministry that ran the monopoly for the government, had made a series of raids that left Lucarelli's operation hurting and vulnerable. And one of the other cigarette smugglers in the city, a long-time rival of Lucarelli's named Gambresca, had seen his chance and ordered two unsuccessful attempts on Lucarelli's life. With the Guardia de Finanza and the local *carabinieri* preparing to make an arrest on one side, and Gambresca and his group devouring what was left of Lucarelli's empire on the other, Lucarelli had been forced to abandon his palace-house and most of his possessions and to go into hiding. The woman, Rita, his mistress of several years, was the only person he'd taken with him.

If he hadn't waited so long he would have been able to get out of Italy on his own; he'd amassed a fortune in smuggling profits, most of which he'd brought with him in cash. But with the heat on from both sides, he'd been afraid to trust former friends and allies and afraid to chance any known escape routes. So, out of desperation, he'd gotten word to Guiseppe Piombo, Carmody's Italian contact in Rome. It was costing him $25,000 for Carmody's services, and it was cheap at the price. Lucarelli knew it too. If Carmody had been a gouger, he could have asked and gotten twice as much.

It was Piombo who had brought in Gino Della Robbia. Carmody needed a man in Venice who knew the city, knew people both reliable and close-mouthed, and Piombo said Della Robbia was that man. The recommendation was good enough for Carmody, but he still hadn't entrusted Della Robbia with Lucarelli's name, the location of the San Spirito house, or any except essential details. No one other than Piombo had that information. The fewer people who knew, the less chance there was of something screwing up.

Della Robbia had proved capable, and now all the details were set. They would take Vickers' boat straight down the Adriatic and into the Mediterranean, then swing around Sicily and go up to the southern coast of Sardinia to the port of Cagliari. Lucarelli wanted to live in an Italian-speaking area, and the rich man's playground of Sardinia was a good place to get lost if you had enough money, a new name, and a new background that would stand up to any but the sharpest scrutiny. Carmody had made arrangements for a villa outside Cagliari and a set of forged papers that included a marriage license and new passports. After they reached Sicily, what happened to Lucarelli and his mistress was up to them.

Lucarelli drank from his fresh glass of wine, worked his mustache over, looked at the map again. "What time do we leave tonight?" he asked.

"I'll meet the launch at ten," Carmody told him. "It shouldn't take more than half an hour to get here, so we'll figure on ten-thirty as the pick-up time. Another half-hour to get to the *Piraeus*. We'll be on our way out of the Lagoon not much after eleven."

"We wear dark clothing?"

"That's right. But keep it simple—and not all black. We don't want to look like a commando team."

"Just as you say, *signor*."

Carmody got to his feet, refolded the map, put it away inside his jacket. "If anything comes up that you should know about, I'll notify you. Otherwise be ready at ten-thirty."

Lucarelli nodded.

From the chair across the room, Rita spoke for the first time. "I cannot stay in this house another night. This waiting . . . it makes me crazy."

"Tonight, *dulce mia*," Lucarelli said to her. "The plans will not change. Tonight we leave, Saturday we are on Sardinia. Yes, Signor Carmody?"

"That's how it shapes up," Carmody said. "Just hang loose. And remember what I said about the wine. If you're even half-drunk when I get here, we don't go."

In his room at the Saviola, a renovated sixteenth-century palace that was one of the more comfortable hotels along the Grand Canal, Carmody called Della Robbia. "It's tonight," he said. "Get in touch with Vickers, tell him to be three hundred yards off the Quartieri Vergini, opposite the clock tower, at least twenty minutes before eleven."

"*Sí*, Signor Carmody."

"And tell your launch driver to pick me up at ten sharp, just where you told him. Make sure he understands ten sharp."

"It will be done."

"Call me if there are any problems."

"There will be no problems."

"I hope not. As soon as I'm paid in full, I'll wire your money to you care of Piombo."

"*Bene*," Della Robbia said.

Carmody lay back on the bed with one of his cigars

and waited for it to be time to move out.

In the shadows at the foot of Via Giordano, Carmody stood looking for the launch. The night was dark, moonless, hushed except for the faint pulsing sounds of water traffic on the Grand Canal. An occasional black gondola glided past on the Rio di Fontego a few feet away, but the area was as deserted as he'd estimated it would be. It was just ten o'clock.

He wore dark trousers, a dark shirt, his Beretta in its half-holster under his jacket. His bag rested at his feet; he had checked out of the Saviola two hours ago. Supper had killed an hour and a quarter, and he'd spent the rest of the time in a water taxi and on foot from the Rialto Bridge.

He looked at his watch again—10:01—and when he lowered his arm he heard the muffled throb of a boat engine. Seconds later the launch, small and radio-equipped like the water taxis, came along the *rio* and drifted over to the seawall. The man behind the wheel starboard called softly, "*Signor?*"

Carmody looked back along Via Giordano, saw nothing to worry him, and came out of the shadows. He descended the three steps cut into the seawall, boarded the launch, stowed his bag under the front seat. The driver—bearded, wearing a beret and a black turtleneck—kept his eyes on the canal, waiting for instructions.

Carmody said, "Rio San Spirito. Number fifty-two. Can you find it?"

"San Spirito? Yes, I know it."

"Let's go then."

The darkness was thick in the narrow canals through which they maneuvered; half the time the red-and-green running lights on the launch was the only illumination. Most of the ancient, decaying buildings along the *riis* were dark. Even the occupied ones had shutters drawn across their oblong windows that allowed little light to escape. Carmody watched astern, but the only other crafts were an occasional taxi or a wraithlike gondola gliding into or out of one of the maze of waterways. The silence, broken only by the throb of the launch's inboard, was as heavy as the odor of garbage and salt water.

It was not quite ten-thirty when the driver brought them into the black mouth of another canal and said, "San Spirito, *signor.*"

Carmody looked for familiar landmarks, found one. "Fifty-two is the first building on the near side of that bridge ahead."

The driver cut power, eased the launch in close to the unbroken line of brick-and-cement walls on the right. When they neared the small arched bridge Carmody pointed out the landing platform beyond number fifty-two. The launch drifted up to it. Carmody waited until the driver held steady, then jumped onto the platform.

"Wait here," he said to the driver. "And keep the engine running."

The canal door to Lucarelli's building was at the near end of the seawall, set into the right-angled corner between the *rio* and a high garden wall made of brick. Carmody went there, used a corroded brass knocker.

"Carmody. Open up."

There was the sound of a bolt being shot, then a key turning in the old-fashioned latch. The door edged inward. Carmody went inside, and Lucarelli was standing three feet away with a pistol in his hand. The muzzle dipped when Carmody stopped and stared at him. He said nervously, "All is well, Signor Carmody?"

Carmody took a close look at him. Lucarelli's breath smelled of wine but he was sober enough. Barely.

He said, "Put that gun away," and moved down the hallway into the room where they had talked that afternoon. Three large leather suitcases sat on the floor next to the table. Carmody thought that the biggest of them would contain Lucarelli's run-out money, from which he'd be paid when they reached Sardinia.

The woman, Rita, stood next to the suitcases. She said,

"We are leaving now?" in her thickly accented English. She was even twitchier than she had been earlier; she couldn't seem to keep her hands still.

"We're leaving," Carmody told her.

Lucarelli came into the room plucking at his bare upper lip. The pistol was tucked away in his clothing. He and Rita gathered up the suitcases so Carmody could keep his hands free. He went ahead of them to the door, looked out. The launch sat silently against the platform, the driver waiting at the wheel; as much of San Spirito as he could see was deserted. Carmody stepped out, motioned to Lucarelli and the woman. While the suitcases were being handed into the launch, he stood apart and shifted his gaze back and forth along the canal.

The woman said suddenly in Italian, "My cosmetic case. I left it inside." Her voice seemed high and shrill in the stillness. She moved away, back toward the still-open door to the building.

"Wait, Rita . . ." Lucarelli began, but she had her back to him, almost to the door now.

And in that moment Carmody sensed, rather than saw, the first movement in the shadows beyond the bridge.

The muscles in his neck and shoulders went tight. He swept his jacket back, slid the Beretta out of its holster. The shadows seemed to separate, like an amoeba reproducing, and a formless shape slipped away from the seawall, coming under the bridge. There was the faint pulsation of a boat engine.

Carmody shouted, "Lucarelli! Get down!"

He dropped to one knee, sighted at the moving shape of the boat as it drew nearer, fired twice. One of the bullets broke glass somewhere on the boat; the other missed wide, hit the cement wall across the canal. Then a man-shape reared up at the wheel, and the night erupted in bright chattering flashes. Bullets sprayed the platform, the launch.

None of them hit Carmody because he was already in the canal.

The water was chill, as black and thick as ink; he could taste the pollution of it, the foulness of oil and garbage. He kicked straight down, at an angle across the narrow width of the *rio*. The Beretta was still in his hand; he shoved it inside the waistband of his trousers before struggling out of his jacket. Swimming blind, groping ahead of him for the wall on the far side, the pressure mounting in his lungs . . . and then his fingers came in contact with the rough surface. He crawled upward along it and poked his head out of the water, dragging air through his mouth, looking back.

The ambush boat had drawn alongside the launch. The dark form of the shooter was hurriedly transferring Lucarelli's suitcases into his own craft, his other hand still clutching a bulky machine pistol. A long way off, somebody was yelling. There was intermittent light along the canal now, but not enough for Carmody to tell if the boat held just the one man or if there was a back-up as well.

The shooter pulled the last suitcase aboard. Turning, he saw Carmody along the far wall. Carmody dove deep as the machine pistol came up and began to chatter again; none of the slugs touched him. Near the bottom he kicked back across the canal to the other side.

Above him, he heard the boat's engine grow loud; the water churned. The shooter wasn't wasting any more time. He didn't want to be seen and he didn't want to risk running into a police boat. By the time Carmody crawled up along the seawall and surfaced again, the ambush boat was a dark blob just swinging out of San Spirito into another canal.

There were more lights showing in nearby buildings, people with their heads stuck out between partially opened shutters. Carmody swam to the launch, caught the port gunwale, hauled himself up and inside.

Lucarelli hadn't reacted quickly enough; he lay dead in the stern, stitched across the abdomen with enough bullets to nearly cut him in two. The driver had been shot twice in the throat. The launch's deck was slick with blood.

Stop worrying, Lucarelli, I'll get you safely to Sardinia. I've never lost a client yet. Leave everything to me . . .

Impotent rage made Carmody's head ache malignantly. He looked under the front seat, saw that his own suitcase was still there. He pushed it onto the platform, climbed up after it, ran with it to the door of number fifty-two. Inside, he went through the three downstairs rooms and two upstairs, checked inside the bathroom and the closets.

The house was empty.

The woman, Rita, was gone.

Carmody went out a side door into a garden grown wild with wisteria and oleander. The windows of an adjacent building looked down into it, and a fat man in an undershirt stood framed in one, shouting querulously. Three big chestnut trees grew in the garden's center; Carmody stayed in their shadow until he found a gate opening onto one of the narrow interior streets.

As he came running through the gate, a tall youth materialized from the darkness in front of him, lured by the excitement. Carmody didn't want his face seen; he lowered his shoulder, sent the kid sprawling against the garden wall. He ran to the first corner, turned it into another street, ran another block, turned a second corner and came out in a *campiello* with a small stone statue in its center.

He ducked around the statue, went into an alley on the opposite side of the square. With his back against the alley wall, he watched the *campiello* to see if he had pursuit. No one came into it. He stayed where he was for a couple of minutes, catching his breath, shivering inside his wet clothing. Then he moved deeper into the blackness, set his bag down, worked the catches to open it.

Rita, he was thinking, it had to have been Rita.

Besides Piombo and himself—and Piombo could be trusted—the woman and Lucarelli were the only ones who knew about the San Spirito house. And she'd gone back into the house, out of harm's way, just seconds before the shooting started. And the shooter? Lucarelli's rival, Gambresca, or somebody sent by him. She'd found some way to tip Gambresca. For money, or hatred, or revenge, or a combination of all three. Money was part of Gambresca's motive, for sure: the shooter had taken the time to fish the three suitcases out of the launch, so he had to have known what one of them contained.

But why had they done it that way? Why not just put a knife in Lucarelli at the house and walk out with the money? Or tip Gambresca days sooner? They'd been living on San Spirito for more than a week. Maybe she wasn't up to the job of cold-blooded murder herself, or maybe it had taken her all this time to work up the courage for a doublecross, or maybe Lucarelli had had the money hidden in a place only he knew about. Whatever the reason, it was incidental.

Rita and Gambresca—they were what mattered.

While all of this was going through his mind Carmody changed clothes in the darkness. The sodden things went into the suitcase, rolled into a towel. The Beretta went into the pocket of the Madras jacket he now wore.

He left the alley, hunted around until he found a tavern. Inside, locked in the toilet, he broke down the Beretta and cleaned and oiled it with materials from the false bottom of his bag. When he was satisfied that it was in working order he went out into the bar proper and drank two cognacs to get the taste of the canal water out of his mouth.

There was a telephone on the rear wall. Carmody called Della Robbia's number. As soon as he heard the Italian's voice he said, "Carmody. Bad trouble. The whole thing's blown."

Silence for a couple of seconds. Then Della Robbia said, "What happened, *signor?*"

"We were ambushed. The man I was taking out is dead. So's your launch driver. One man waiting for us in a boat with a machine pistol—maybe a back-up. It was too dark to see much."

"*Cacchio!*"

"Yeah. A big pile of shit."

"You are all right, Signor Carmody?"

"No physical wounds," Carmody said bitterly. He was holding the phone receiver as if it were the shooter's neck. "Listen, I need you and your connections. The man I was taking out was Renzo Lucarelli. You know him?"

"Lucarelli? Yes . . . yes, of course."

"He had a woman, Rita, who was supposed to go with us. But she ducked off just before we got hit. I think she's a Judas."

"Why would she—?"

Carmody said, "I don't have all the answers yet—that's what I need you for. You know anything about this Rita?"

"Very little, *signor.* Almost nothing."

"How about a rival of Lucarelli's named Gambresca?"

"A bad one," Della Robbia said. "You believe Gambresca was involved in the shooting?"

"That's how it looks. You know where I can find him?"

"A moment, Signor Carmody, I must think. Yes. He owns a wholesale produce company on Campo Oroglia. It is said he lives above it."

"All right," Carmody said. "Find out what you can about the woman. She may be with Gambresca, she may not be. I want her, Della Robbia, and I want her before she can get out of Venice. Lucarelli is the first client I ever lost and I won't stand still for it."

"I will do what I can," Della Robbia said. "Where are you? Where can I—?"

"I'll be in touch," Carmody told him and rang off.

He tried to find out from the bartender how to get to the nearest canal that had water taxi service. The bartender didn't speak English. None of the drinkers spoke English. Carmody's Italian was weak; it took him five long, impatient minutes to get directions that made sense.

When he went out again into the night he was running.

There was nobody home at Gambresca's.

Carmody stepped out from under the doorway arch, looked up once more at the sign running across the top of the warehouse. It said *A. Gambresca* in broad black lettering, and below that: *Campo Oroglia 24.* His gaze moved higher, to the dark windows strung along the second floor front. No sign of life. He had been there for several minutes, ringing bells and making noise like a drunk, his fingers restless on the Beretta in his jacket pocket. There hadn't been any response.

Carmody looked at his watch. Almost one-thirty. He crossed the square to enter the same street by which he'd arrived, his steps echoing hollowly in the late-night stillness. The fury inside him boiled like water in a kettle.

What now? Another call to Della Robbia. And if Della Robbia hadn't found out anything? The waiting game, like it or not. He would pick a vantage point somewhere on Campo Oroglia, and he would sit there all night if necessary, until Gambresca showed up.

In the lobby of a small hotel nearby he gave a sleepy night clerk a thousand-lire note for the use of his telephone. Della Robbia answered immediately.

Carmody said, "Well?"

"I have learned something, but perhaps it means little or nothing."

"I'll decide that. What is it?"

"The woman has an uncle, a man named Salviati, who owns a *squero*—a boatyard for the repair and construction of gondolas. The uncle is said to have smuggled contraband and has two boats of high speed at his disposal. It is possible the woman has gone there."

Carmody gave it some thought. Yes, possible. Assuming it was the money that had driven her to sell out Lucarelli, she might have already got her payoff and then headed for her uncle's—a place to hide or a way to leave the city, either one. She'd need someone she could trust, and Gambresca might not be that someone. Another possibility was that she'd gone to the uncle straight from San Spirito, to wait for Gambresca or one of Gambresca's people to bring her blood money.

He asked, "Where is this place, this *squero?*"

"On Rio degli Zecchini."

"So I can get there by water taxi."

"If you can find one at this hour."

"I can find one," Carmody said.

From where he stood in the shadows across the Rio degli Zecchini, Carmody could see the vague shapes of gondolas, some whole and some skeletal, in the *squero's* low-fenced rear yard. Set back fifty feet from the canal was a two-story, wood-and-brick building that looked as if it had been built in the time of the Doges; it was completely dark. Most of the surrounding buildings were warehouses and the area was deserted. No light showed anywhere except for a pale streetlamp atop a canal bridge nearby.

Carmody put his suitcase into a wall niche, took out the Beretta, held it cupped low against his right leg as he walked to the bridge. On the opposite seawall he stood listening for a time. A ship's horn bayed mournfully on the Lagoon; the canal water, rumpled by the wind, lapped at the seawall. There were no sounds of any kind from the *squero.*

The place's rear entrance was a wooden gate set into a three-sided frame of two-by-fours; the fourth side was the wall of the adjacent building. On the canal side, and on top, the beams sprouted tangles of barbed wire like a fungoid growth. Carmody had had experience with barbed wire before, but he still cut the palm of his left hand in two places when he swung around the frame. The sharp sting of the cuts heaped fuel on his rage.

Moving quickly, he made his way across the yard. The gondolas—long, slender, flat-bottomed, with tapered and upswept prow and stern—were laid out in rows, on davits, in stacks of two and three; they had a ghostly look in the darkness, like giant bones in a graveyard. They also camouflaged his run to the far corner of the building, in case anybody happened to be looking out.

Jalousied shutters were lowered across the double-doored entrance; there were no fronting windows. Carmody edged around the corner, along the side wall. An elongated window halfway down showed him nothing of the interior, just a solid screen of blackness.

Carmody paused, peering toward the back. A high wall marked the rear boundary of the *squero* but it was set several feet beyond the building, forming a narrow passageway. He went there and into the passage; picked his way through a carpeting of refuse, looking for another window. Midway along he found one with louvered shutters closed across it. He squinted upward through one of the canted louvers.

Light.

Movement.

Carmody bent lower so he could see more of the room inside. It was an office of sorts, with a cluttered desk on which a gooseneck lamp burned, two wooden chairs, a table piled with charts and pamphlets, a filing cabinet with a rusted fan on top.

And the woman, Rita.

She stood to one side of the desk, in profile, nervously watching the closed door opposite the window. Her arms were folded across her heavy breasts, as if she were cold; her face was drawn, bloodless. Between her lips was a filter-tipped cigarette that she smoked in short, deep drags.

Carmody glided back the way he'd come, stopped before the unshuttered window at the front part of the building. It was the kind that opened inward on a pair of hinges, with a simple slip catch locking it to the frame. He went to work with the broad flat blade of his Swiss Army knife. After two minutes he put the tips of his fingers against the dirty glass, cautiously pushed the window open.

The interior smelled of paint and linseed oil and dampness. Carmody climbed over the sill, stood motionless on a rough concrete floor. He could see where the door to the office was by a strip of light at its bottom. He could also make out a lathe, a drill press, a table saw, several wood forms, all massed up in the blackness — an obstacle course for him to get through without making any noise.

Slowly, feeling in front of him with his left hand, he moved toward the strip of light. He had to detour twice, the second time abruptly to keep from colliding with a sawhorse. When he reached the door he stopped to listen. She was quiet in there, and since she'd been watching the door minutes earlier, it figured that she was still watching it. He had no way of knowing whether or not she was armed. He hadn't seen a gun, but he'd only had a limited view of the office.

He wrapped his left hand around the knob, twisted it, then threw his left shoulder against the door. The latch was open; the door banged against the table inside, dislodging papers. The woman let out a shriek and stumbled away from the desk, one hand going to her mouth. Her eyes were like buttons about to pop from too much pressure.

Carmody got to her in three long strides, caught her dark hair in his free hand, spun her around and sat her down hard in one of the chairs. Then he knelt in front of her, his angry face less than six inches from hers, and laid the Beretta's muzzle against her cheek.

He could see that she wanted to scream again, but nothing came out when she opened her mouth. Her eyes rolled up in their sockets. Carmody slapped her twice, hard. The blows refocused her vision, brought her out of the faint before she had really gone into it.

She stared at him with a mixture of shock and terror. "Signor Carmody . . ."

"That's right — alive and well."

"But you . . . I believed . . ."

"I know what you believed," he said thinly. "But I was luckier than Lucarelli and the boat driver. Where's the money? And where's Gambresca?"

"Gambresca! That *stronzolo*, he was the one . . ."

"You ought to know, you sold us out to him."

She blinked. "I do not understand."

"The hell you don't understand."

"I was so afraid," she whispered. She was trembling now. "I did not wish to die. This is why I run away. Please, I know nothing about Gambresca."

"Are you trying to tell me you didn't set up that ambush?"

"Ambush?"

"The boat, the shooting."

"No! How could I? You cannot think—"

"Why did you run back to the house just before the shooting started?"

"My *cosmeticos*, I forget them."

"Sure you did."

"I tell the truth! Renzo was my man, we go away together, you cannot think I want him to die!"

"Somebody wanted him to die," Carmody said. "Somebody tipped Gambresca. And you and Lucarelli were the only ones besides me and my man in Rome who knew where the hideaway was. You did it for the money, right? For a cut of the run-out money?"

"No, no, no! I did not, I would not . . ."

She was shaking her head, forgetting the gun at her cheek; Carmody pulled the Beretta back a little. It was quiet in the office just then—and in that quiet he heard the faint sound of a footfall in the darkness out front.

The hackles raised on his neck. He came up off his knee, turning, and when he did that he saw the vague shape of a man appear next to the drill press out there, just beyond the outspill of light from the desk lamp. In the man's hand was a familiar, deadly shape.

Carmody threw himself to one side, pushing Rita and the chair over backwards. She screamed again but the sound of it was lost in the stuttering roar of the machine pistol. A slug ripped through the tail of Carmody's jacket, burned across one buttock. Then the gooseneck lamp flew off the desk, shattered, and the office went dark except for bright flashes from the pistol's muzzle.

Carmody managed to get the desk between himself
and the doorway. He could hear the rap, rap, rap of the
bullets digging into the desk, into the wall above him, as
the shooter raked the office with another burst. He twisted
his body into the kneehole. He could see out on the other
side, but without the muzzle flashes the darkness was too
thick for him to locate the shooter. The air stank of burnt
gunpowder; the silence had an electric quality. Carmody
listened, knowing that the shooter was listening too.

The silence seemed to gain magnitude until it was
almost deafening. Either the shooter didn't know where
the overhead lights were or he didn't want to take the
chance of putting them on. But with the amount of slugs
he'd pumped into the office, he had to be thinking that
he was the only one left alive. If he'd opened up with that
MAC-10 two seconds earlier he'd have been right.

Pretty soon there was a series of scuffling sounds out
beyond the doorway. Carmody still didn't move. They were
the kinds of sounds somebody makes when he's pretending
to leave a place, trying to be clever. The shooter was still
out there, waiting. Making up his mind.

Another couple of minutes crawled away. The quiet
was so intense it was like a humming in Carmody's ears.
Then there was a nearly inaudible sliding sound: the
shooter was moving again. Not going away this time.
Coming back into the office.

Carmody steadied the Beretta on his left arm.

Nothing happened for a few seconds. Then there was
another faint, whispery footfall. And another, not more
than ten feet away and almost directly ahead—

Carmody emptied most of the Beretta's clip on a line
waist-high and two feet wide.

There was a half-strangled Italian oath; a moment later
Carmody heard the metallic clatter of the pistol on concrete, the sound of a body falling heavily. He stayed where
he was, listening. A scrabbling movement, a low moan
. . . nothing.

It was another couple of minutes before he was

satisfied. He crawled out of the kneehole, got to his feet, moved at an angle to the door. He put his pencil flash on, just for an instant, stepping aside as he did so. Then the tension went out of him and he put the light on again, left it on.

The shooter was lying half in and half out of the office doorway, the MAC-10 alongside him. Face down, not moving. Carmody turned him over with the toe of one shoe, shined the light on his face—on the dead, staring eyes.

Gino Della Robbia.

Carmody swore softly. He wasn't surprised; nothing surprised him any more. But that didn't make Della Robbia's treachery any easier to take.

He swung the light to the rear of the office, located Rita with it. At first he thought she was dead too because she lay crumpled and still. But when he went over there and knelt beside her, he saw that she was breathing. Blood glistened on the side of her head: scalp wound. He didn't see any others. She was lucky. They both were—damned lucky.

He found the switch for the overheads, flipped it on. Then he picked Rita up and sat her in a chair. The movement brought her out of it. For a couple of minutes she was disoriented, hysterical; he slapped her face, got her calmed down. Then she saw Della Robbia and that almost set her off again.

When she could talk she said, "Gino? It was Gino who killed Renzo?"

"And tried to kill me," Carmody said. "Twice."

"But I do not understand . . ."

"It's simple enough. Gambresca had nothing to do with the ambush, just like you had nothing to do with it. Della Robbia, nobody else. For the money. He didn't know how much there was but he did know that it would be plenty— enough to take the risks he took."

She shook her head, winced, sat still.

Carmody said, "You went to him tonight after the ambush, didn't you? Heard me mention his name to Lucarelli, remembered it, looked up his address and went to him."

"Yes. I believed you and Renzo were both dead. I had nowhere else to go."

"And he got you to come here."

"Yes."

"What'd he say to you?"

"That this was the *squero* of a friend. That I should wait here. He gave me a key."

"Wait for what?"

"For him to come. He said he would help me leave Venezia."

Carmody nodded. He was thinking that Della Robbia must have been in a hell of a sweat when he got home from San Spirito and one of the men he thought he'd killed called him on the phone—the one man he should have made sure died first. If he could have found out where Carmody was, he'd have gone there to finish the job. But Carmody hadn't told him and Della Robbia had been afraid to force the issue. So he'd sweated some more and waited for the next call. Then Rita had showed up and he'd thought of this *squero*—the perfect set-up for another ambush. Except that this time he'd been the one who got caught in it.

One question remained: How had Della Robbia found out where Lucarelli's hideout was? Piombo wouldn't have told him. The launch hadn't been followed tonight; Carmody had made sure of that. And he hadn't been followed on any of the previous trips he'd made to Rio San Spirito.

Only one possible answer—one that Carmody should have thought of at the Rio di Fontego tonight. By overlooking the possibility, he had gotten Lucarelli killed and almost lost his own life. Unforgiveable. He would never forget this mistake, and he would never make another like it again.

The answer, the oversight, was that the launch had

been equipped with a shortwave radio. Della Robbia must have bribed the driver to open the microphone just before he picked Carmody up, so that when Carmody told him where they were going, Della Robbia had heard the address on a radio on his own boat tuned to the same band. Easy enough then to take a different and quicker route to San Spirito, hide and wait.

Carmody prodded Rita onto her feet, led her through the building and outside. The area was still deserted. It would take a while to find transportation at this hour, but that was a minor inconvenience.

Rita said, "Where are we going, Signor Carmody?"

"Della Robbia's house. Odds are that's where the money is."

"You will keep it all for yourself? The money?"

"No. It's yours—you've earned the right to it. All I want is the fee Lucarelli and I agreed on."

"You . . . you mean this?"

"I mean it," Carmody said. "This too: If you still want to go to Sardinia, I'll take you there. I don't like to leave a job unfinished."

"Yes, I want to go. Oh yes."

"It might take another day or two to rearrange things but I'll find a safe place for you to wait. It won't be too bad."

She looked at him with her large dark eyes. "No," she said, "I do not think it will be bad at all."

A RUN IN DIAMONDS

SATURDAY MORNING – CARMODY

Carmody sat waiting on the patio of Pepé's Spanish Bar, drinking an iced San Miguel and watching the water skiers out on the Mediterranean. It was a half hour before noon on a Saturday in July—very hot on the patio, as it always was on the island of Majorca in the summer. Sweat glistened on his leathery face, on his chest under his unbuttoned silk shirt.

He drank the last of his beer, motioned down toward the air-conditioned interior of Pepé's until he caught the eye of the day bartender, Antonio. Then he let his gaze wander over the solidly packed beach that stretched from Palma Nova to Magalluf. Bright-colored sun chairs made of plastic weave with little square hoods were arranged in uneven rows that followed the *playa's* curve; in them and around them were the flocks of tourists from Britain and northern Europe—the wealthy and pseudo-wealthy who would be staying in the modern stone-and-glass high-rise hotels for their two or three weeks; the secretaries and the career women and the sun-and-fun types who would be sharing rooms in the smaller hotels set far back from the beach, or maybe shacking up with one of the local studs because it was even cheaper that way; the honeymooners and social climbers and grocery-money savers; the old and the young, the beautiful and the desperate, the shrewd and the stupid.

Seagulls, Carmody thought, as he always did when he was aware of them. Fluttering and pecking and nodding, some in the water and some out of it, some looking for scavengings and some for nothing at all—making meaningless cawing sounds in the broiling sun.

Antonio brought his second beer, went away again. Carmody sat sipping it, waiting and watching the tourists. Inevitably one of the women—golden-haired, very tall— reminded him of Chana and he stopped watching her and the rest of them and looked out over the Mediterranean again.

Six years now since she'd left him, five years since she'd divorced him. Her fault, he'd thought at first, but it wasn't. Neither of them was to blame. He couldn't change, not even for her; she couldn't accept the life he had made for himself, couldn't adapt to it, not even for him. She'd feared constantly for his safety. And she had an ingrained moral streak that wouldn't allow her to feel comfortable or secure with his profession, even though she'd known what he was and what he did when she married him. It was a marriage that was doomed from the beginning, that he should never have permitted to happen.

But he still loved her, still wanted her; he knew that he always would. No other woman had ever meant anything to him, before or since. He'd had his share of sexual partners over the past six years, but he couldn't remember what any of them looked like or what their names had been. Not even the last one two weeks ago. Not even her nationality or where he had picked her up.

He didn't know where Chana was now, or if she was

remarried. Sometimes he hoped she was but mostly he hoped she wasn't; he wanted her to be happy, to have the family she'd always wanted, but the thought of her in bed with another man ripped at him like claws. He'd made no effort to find out where she'd gone after she left Majorca, or what she'd gone to; he never would. He was afraid of what he might do if he knew—not to Chana, not to any man she might be with, but to himself.

The second bottle of San Miguel was empty when the woman finally showed up. Carmody saw her coming up the stairs from the promenade, knew immediately she was his prospective client. Tall and lithe, this one, with dark hair and high cheekbones and yellow-brown eyes that reminded him of a cat's. Wearing a white dress with a hem that ended an inch below the apex of legs almost as long as Chana's. He judged her to be in her early twenties.

She saw him, and her cat's eyes stayed on him as she approached his table, measuring him warily like an alley female approaching an unfamiliar tom. She was nervous, very nervous; it was in the stiff way she held herself, the little nibbles her teeth kept making at her lower lip. And in her voice when she said, "Are you Carmody?"

American, he thought. Midwest somewhere. He said, "Yes."

"I'm Gillian Waltham."

"You're also twenty minutes late."

"I couldn't help it. The traffic from Palma . . ."

"I don't like to be kept waiting."

"Well, I'm sorry."

"Sorry buys you nothing in this world."

"What?"

"Let it go," Carmody said. "Sit down."

She sat and crossed her good legs, giving him a look at her silk-encased crotch before tugging the hem of the dress down. It might have been accidental, and then again it might not have been. She didn't say anything. Just sat there, nibble, nibble, nibble, looking indecisive.

Carmody said, "So you want to go to Amsterdam."

"Yes. Just for a day . . . two at the most."

"And you don't want to go alone."

"No."

"Then what?"

"After Amsterdam, you mean?"

"After Amsterdam."

"I want to disappear," she said. Her gaze moved restlessly around the patio. "Without any traces."

"Yes?" Carmody said.

"It doesn't matter where."

"You just want to disappear."

"That's what I said, isn't it?"

He ran one of his big, knotty hands through his hair. His flat eyes studied her. She didn't look like the kind of woman who would want to disappear—but then, not too many people looked like what they were or what went on inside them. Faces and bodies were like mummer's masks: they hid men and women from each other.

He said, "How did you get my name?"

"From a friend in the south of France."

"Which friend would that be?"

"Virgil Franklin."

"I don't know anybody named Virgil Franklin."

"Well, Alvarez knows him," the woman said. "They worked together once or twice. In Lisbon."

Alvarez was Carmody's Barcelona contact. He'd spent some time in Lisbon in the fifties, smuggling contraband in and out of Tangier and Casablanca, selling minor secrets to whichever side had the most cash. Carmody didn't particularly like him—he was a pimp now, among other things, and Carmody had never had any use for pimps—but so far Alvarez had never sent him a bad apple or screwed up a deal. Results were what mattered, not personal feelings.

Carmody said, "So you've been living in the south of France."

"Yes."

"Where?"

"Cannes."

"Is that where you got the stones?"

"The what?"

"The diamonds."

She had her purse open and was poking around inside. Sunlight glinted off a dangly silver bracelet on her left wrist. She came out with a package of French cigarettes, lit one with a silver lighter. She exhaled the word "Yes" along with a plume of smoke.

"How hot are they?"

"Hot?"

"When were they stolen?"

"Yesterday."

"By you?"

"Yes."

"From?"

"A man named Jacques Amateaux."

"Who would he be?"

"A retired industrialist. From Pais. He has a large collection of diamonds and other precious gems."

"Does he know the diamonds you took are gone?"

"I suppose he does by now."

"Does he know you're the thief?"

"He will when he finds me gone."

"How influential is he?"

"Very," Gillian said. "He's also ruthless."

"So you think he'll do more than just go to the police."

"He won't go to the police at all."

"No? Why not?"

"He just won't."

"Thief himself, is that it? Big-time?"

"I . . . don't know for sure. But, yes, I think so."

"How many diamonds?"

"Five."

"Worth how much?"

"I don't know exactly. I'm going to get a lot less than their actual value . . ."

"Don't play games with me," Carmody said. "I need to

know what we're dealing with here."

Now she was nibbling on the filter of her cigarette. "They're worth about a hundred and seventy-five thousand dollars on the open market."

Carmody wasn't impressed. At five times that amount he wouldn't have been impressed. He said, "How much are you getting?"

"A hundred thousand."

"That's not bad. Who's your buyer in Amsterdam?"

"A man named Zaanhof."

"I don't know him. Does he do anything else besides fence?"

"Fence?"

"Buy and sell stolen goods," Carmody said impatiently. She was either naive as hell or pretending to be. "Professional or amateur?"

"Professional. He specializes in diamonds."

"How did you get his name?"

"From Virgil Franklin."

"Virgil must be a wealth of information. How do you know him?"

"We . . . I used to see him. When I made up my mind to take the diamonds I asked him some discreet questions. I knew he'd been involved with . . ." She let the sentence trail off.

"Does this Zaanhof have your hundred thousand in hand or is he raising it?"

"He's raising it," Gillian said. "That's why we might be in Amsterdam two days. But there won't be any problem."

"You're certain of that, are you?"

"Zaanhof assured me there won't be."

"When people assure you of something," Carmody said, "that's the time to start worrying. Do you have them with you?"

"The diamonds?"

"What else are we talking about here?"

She sighed out more smoke, crushed the butt of her cigarette in the table ashtray. Without looking at him she said, "They're sewn into the bra I'm wearing."

"Yes?"

"Do you want to see them?" Still not looking at him, but with a hint of defiance in her voice.

"Not right now. Later, when you change bras."

That brought her eyes back to his. Most of her nervousness was gone now. She looked vulnerable and a little frightened. Maybe she was; and maybe that too was part of a mummer's mask. She said, "Then you'll help me?"

"For ten percent of your hundred thousand," Carmody said. "Plus the price of my plane fare both ways and any other expenses."

"Is that all?" She was trying to be sarcastic.

"That's all."

"Very well, then."

"Alvarez said you can give me five thousand now."

"I have it with me, yes."

"Hand it over."

She produced an envelope from her purse. Carmody put in his lap, opened it, riffled through the hundred-dollar bills it contained. "All right. When do you want to leave?"

"As soon as we can. This afternoon, if that's possible."

"It's possible," he told her.

SATURDAY NIGHT – CARMODY

Carmody said, "We'd like a double room, with bath, on the canal side."

Gillian looked sharply at him but said nothing. Purse-lipped, she studied some of the marble statuary adorning the ornate lobby.

The concierge said, "Yes, sir. Will the sixth floor be acceptable?"

"That's fine." Carmody gave him a twenty-gulden note. "We don't want to be disturbed at any time, by anyone, for any reason."

"As you wish, Mr. Carmody."

They were in the Beatrix Hotel, near the Rembrandt-splein in downtown Amsterdam. It was an old hotel, fashioned of reddish-brown brick and stuffed with relics of another age: seven floors of Flemish *haute grandeur*. Carmody had stayed there before. He liked the Beatrix because the staff was discreet, not because of the luxurious trappings.

In the elevator Gillian stood apart from him, kept her eyes to the front. Her lips remained pursed. Christ, Carmody thought, she's miffed about the double room. Why? If the story she'd told him was true, she had to have been sleeping with this Amateaux, the retired industrialist — and probably, though maybe not at the same time, with Alvarez's friend, Virgil Franklin. So why the virginal act with him, unless her story *wasn't* true? He didn't care if it was or wasn't, as long as it didn't have any effect on the job she'd hired him to do. The other possibility was that there was something about him that turned her off. It wouldn't have been the first time. He didn't care if that was the case either. He'd never forced himself on a woman in his life and he wasn't about to start with Gillian Waltham. Small talk, the chase, bored him; either a woman wanted you or she didn't. And if she didn't, you were a damned fool if you didn't leave her alone.

Their room was big, antique-ridden, with a set of double windows at one end that looked down on the tree-lined Amstel Canal. As soon as the bellboy left with another of Carmody's twenty-gulden notes, Gillian set her handbag down on one of her suitcases and turned to face Carmody. Her cat's eyes were angry now.

She said, "What's the idea of asking for a double room?"

"What do you suppose the idea is?"

"I'm not cheap, Carmody. I'm not some bimbo."

"No?"

"No!"

"No screwing then," Carmody said expressionlessly. "That's too bad. You look like you'd be a pretty good lay."

She flushed. "You have a filthy mouth."

Carmody sat on the nearest bed. "Listen," he said, "I took a double because you're paying me to watch over you. I can do that a hell of a lot better from in here than I can from next door or down the hall. If you don't want to sleep with me, fine. I don't want to sleep with you either. Are you reassured now?"

She didn't know what to say to that. He watched her anger cool, watched her turn and walk to the windows and stand there for a time looking out. Pretty soon she turned and asked him, "What time is it?" in a petulant little voice.

"After eleven."

"Well, I'm tired and I'm going to bed."

"Suit yourself."

She took her overnight bag into the bathroom and shut the door, hard. Carmody heard the click of the lock. He lit one of his thin black cigars, blew smoke at the chandelier. From inside the bathroom there was the sound of the shower being turned on. When he heard that he got up and went to her other suitcase and searched it.

She was traveling pretty light for a woman—but then, she was supposedly on the run. There was a dress, some underthings, hose, a pants suit, two skirts, two blouses, a pair of slacks, a pair of Spanish rope-soled *alpargatas*, a container of Regular Tampax, a box of tissues, a paperback edition of a bestseller about sex in Hollywood, and half a carton of French cigarettes. That was all.

Carmody picked up her handbag, looked inside. No particular order to the contents; the usual jumble. He took the purse to the bed, emptied it upside down, sifted the items around on the quilt. Rattail comb, mirror compact, pair of dark-lensed sunglasses, packet of purse-sized tissues, open package of the same cigarettes that were in the suitcase, her silver lighter, a pen, a plastic bottle of prescription tablets that had been filled at a *farmacia* in Málaga and looked as though they might be tranquilizers, a packet of Spanish aspirin, an address book, three Spanish five-peseta coins, a tourist map of Majorca, a drink menu card with *Bar Emperador, Calle Cristóbal Ortiz 29, Málaga, España* embossed on it, and a brown leather wallet.

He opened the wallet. Four thousand-peseta notes, six hundred-peseta notes, and the five hundred-gulden notes she'd gotten at the Schiphol Aerodrome here. In the card section were a snapshot of two middle-aged people standing in front of a frame house with lots of trees around it; a posed portrait of Gillian in a black sweater and a string of pearls that was probably a high-school graduation photo; and an expired American driver's license made out to Gillian Waltham of Canton, Ohio, with her picture on it.

The address book was a third full. Most of the entries were for men and women living in or around Canton. There was one listing in Spain—for a Liane Butler, on Calle Villalonga in Málaga. There were two listings in Nice and one in Biarritz, but none in Cannes and none for Virgil Franklin or Jacques Amateaux.

The sound of the shower spray stopped. Carmody put the wallet and address book into the handbag, scooped the rest of the stuff inside, brushed flakes of tobacco from the quilt. He put the purse back where he'd found it. Then he sat on the bed again and lit another of his cigars. He was half finished with it when she came out of the bathroom.

Her hair was down now, combed out; it made her look even younger. He could see the outline of her nipples, hardened by the shower, under the thin cotton pajamas she wore. She had the top buttoned to her throat, the tails tucked into the bottom. She looked about eighteen.

Carmody said, "Where's your bra?"

She blinked at him. "What?"

"Your bra. Where is it?"

"In the bathroom."

"Get it. I want to see those diamonds."

Gillian didn't argue. She got the brassiere, threw it on the bed beside him. "The right cup," she said. "Along the top."

He felt where the stones—five of them—were sewn into the band seam. With his knife he cut the stitching, then popped the diamonds out into the palm of his left hand. He studied them for a time, moving them around with the tip of his right index finger. Then he held one up to the light. He was no expert but the gems seemed genuine: baguette-cut, several carats each, with a brilliant surface luster.

91

Gillian said, "Now who's going to sew them back in?"

"Nobody. I'll keep them until we see Zaanhof."

"Now wait a minute—"

"Shut up," he said flatly.

"Why should I? They're *my* diamonds—"

"Yes? I told you before, I don't care how you got them or who you got them from, but I don't like to be lied to. You came from somewhere in Spain—Málaga probably—a hell of a lot sooner than you came from Cannes. If there are any more lies in your story, like about Virgil Franklin and Zaanhof and how much you're getting for the stones, you'd better tell me now. It'll cost you double if I find out about them later on."

She stared at him with her mouth coming open. "You went through my things! Damn you, you had no right to do that!"

"Sure I did. Your lies gave me the right."

"I only lied to you about Cannes; I didn't know if I could trust you. I still don't know. You searched my things and now you want to keep the diamonds."

"You think I'm going to steal them from you?"

"For all I know you might be planning to."

"Well I'm not," Carmody said. "I don't steal from my clients. I don't lie to them either."

"All *right*. I shouldn't have lied, I'm sorry."

"Just about Cannes?"

"I told you, yes."

"Where does Virgil Franklin live?"

"In Málaga."

"Yes? You don't have his name in your address book."

"Why should I? I know where he lives and I don't need to write down his telephone number."

"What about this retired industrialist of yours? Málaga too?"

"Yes. He's Spanish, not French."

"And all you're getting for the diamonds is a hundred thousand dollars, cash?"

"That's all."

"I hope so," Carmody said, "for your sake. But I'll still keep the diamonds until we see Zaanhof."

From his suitcase he took out a small chamois neck pouch with a rawhide band. The diamonds went inside and the pouch went around his neck. Then he began taking off his shirt.

Gillian moved to the other bed, got into it, pulled the covers up around her neck. "Don't you use the bathroom to get undressed, for God's sake?"

"What for?" he said.

He stripped to his shorts, then got his Beretta from the false bottom of the suitcase and put the gun under his pillow. Gillian watched him without speaking, her eyes on his face the whole time. He shut off the lights, slid into bed. He didn't say anything and neither did she. His mind kept working for a while, and he could tell from the irregular sound of the woman's breathing that she was wide awake. He wasn't amused. If she wanted to spend the night lying there waiting for something to happen, that was her business.

Carmody rolled onto his side and went to sleep.

SUNDAY,
LATE AFTERNOON – SILVERA

Diego Silvera arrived in Palma on the afternoon plane from Málaga. As he walked through the airport concourse, he smiled with pleasure. Palma was a beautiful city, Majorca a beautiful island; nearly two years away from them was much too long.

Familiar images flicked across his mind like colored slides: the harbor, Old Town, the Borné, the cathedral and Almudaina Palace, the beaches at Ca'n Pastilla and Calamayor, the nightclubs around Plaza Gomilla in El Terreno . . . ah, Palma was a fine city indeed. When he had completed his work for the *patrón* he would spend a week, perhaps two, at one of the luxury hotels on the Paseo Maritimo. Women were plentiful here; he would have no trouble finding one with the blood of a gypsy to share his holiday.

He was aware of the women who watched him with unconcealed interest as he passed through the lobby and out into the late-afternoon heat. Their approval deepened his pleasure. He was a tall man, handsome, with thick black hair and teeth as white as sun-bleached bones. There was a sensual grace in the way he moved. A great many women found him exciting, intriguing. Men liked him, too, because he did not flaunt his masculinity and they found they could deal with him as an equal even if they were ugly as toads. He laughed often, as a man does when he enjoys life. And he enjoyed life more than most.

He enjoyed it because inside him there was death, and death was as pleasing to him as life.

In the past ten years he had in cold blood and mostly for money killed seventeen men and three women. He had used a knife on seven of the men, and beaten six to death with his fist and a variety of blunt instruments, and shot the other four with his good friend the Browning automatic. He had strangled each of the three women, slowly, while he was having sex with them. Soon he would kill again. And many more times after that. The knowledge was as heady to him as strong, sweet wine.

Truly, Diego Silvera was a happy man.

A taxi took him from the airport to one of the car rental agencies on Calle Aragon in the city proper. There he rented a Spanish Seat 1200 sedan, paying a week in advance from a thick roll of thousand-peseta notes. By way of the Autopista and the Paseo Martimo he drove out of Palma to the west.

After eighteen kilometers on the main Andraitx road, just outside Palma Nova, he spied the secondary road that led toward the villages of Calvia and Capdella. He turned there, drove another three kilometers. On his right, then, an unpaved lane branched upward through pine and uncultivated almond trees. He followed that until it dead-ended at the crest of a hill, in a flat stony clearing.

At the clearing's far end, set at the edge of a steep fall, was a villa constructed of unpainted stone-and-mortar and heavy dark wood. Green louvered shutters were fastened over the windows. A stone-floor patio fronted the villa, set inside knee-high retaining walls.

Silvera brought the Seat to a stop, took the Browning automatic from his carry-all and put it inside his jacket, and left the car. It was quiet here; a feathery breeze playing in the trees was the only sound. Over the tops of the pines he could see the Bahia de Palma at Palma Nova; and behind him, across rolling fields and green valleys, the resort community of Santa Ponsa and more of the Mediterranean; and on his left, inland, the high pine-studded slopes of the mountain range which ran across the island's western peninsula. Silvera smiled. Such a fine view, he thought. Someday he would own a villa with a view equally as impressive. His smile widened; he laughed aloud. Perhaps this very one!

He stepped over the retaining wall, crossed the patio under a huge algarroba tree. The front entrance, of course, was secure. He moved to the rear wall. It was built at the edge of the slope, forming a low extension of the villa's back wall.

Silvera took off his sports jacket, folded it and laid it carefully aside, then climbed onto the stones. A pillar-supported balcony ran the full width of the villa, extending out over the fall by some twenty feet. He caught onto its side railing, stretched his left foot so that it was braced on the nearest support beam, swung himself off the wall and up and over the railing onto the balcony—all in one quick, fluid movement.

The balcony was empty except for a large stone barbecue. The heavy doors into the house were locked; thick drapes kept him from seeing inside through the glass. He went to work with a set of picks. The lock was a good one. It took him nearly fifteen minutes to open it. He went inside, found the pullstring for the drapes, drew them wide.

Waning sunlight brightened a Spartanly furnished room with a fireplace at one end. On a side wall, beneath an oil painting of a sad-eyed Majorcan peasant in a grove of stunted olive trees, stood a portable bar. Silvera went to the bar, spent a few seconds admiring the painting.

Then he looked through the bar stock, chose a bottle of Johnnie Walker Black Label, poured himself a generous drink. Tasting it, he glanced at his wristwatch. It was almost six-thirty.

He found the telephone and called the *patrón* collect, to let him know everything was proceeding according to plan.

MONDAY MORNING – FANNING

Standing at the balcony railing, the sun hot and nourishing on his face, Allen Fanning felt as if he owned the world.

He had handled things nicely here, he thought, quite professionally, as he had handled dozens of other business transactions over the years. Crisp, efficient, revealing only what was necessary and nothing more, coming to terms without difficulty. Jennifer would be pleased when he told her, proud of him. He savored the image of her face and how radiant it was when she was happy.

Jennifer, dear Jennifer. He thought again, with the same sense of wonder, that until he'd met and fell in love with her, nothing of significance had happened in his fifty-one years of living. His childless, loveless marriage to Irene . . . his clerk's jobs in London . . . the decision, after his position with Benson & Sons had ended abruptly through no fault of his own, to take the secretarial job with the retired British colonel in Lisbon . . . the move to Spain and another secretarial job after the colonel's death in 1962. All dull interludes in an uneventful life. All preludes. The ironic thing was that he hadn't even realized how empty his life was. He had a niche, a profession which served him well and saw to his modest needs, and it had made him blind and complacent.

That had all changed six weeks ago in Málaga, on a hot morning just like this one. Fate, kismet, or simple coincidence that he and Jennifer had both decided to take a stroll through the Plaza del General Quiepo de Llano? Not that it mattered. She had come into his world that morning and turned it upside down—dizzingly, wonderfully. And he had been reborn.

With her in his arms, he was a *man* for the first time in his life: virile, powerful, dominant. With her at his side he could do and be anything. The twenty-four-year difference in their ages meant nothing. He loved her as deeply as any man could love any woman; and after their first night together, he knew that he would do whatever it took—whatever it took—to keep her . . .

Fanning took a sip of his gin-and-tonic, looking out over the tops of the pines on the slope below. In the distance, the Bahia de Palma shimmered under the bright sun. Nearly noon. If he left soon and the island traffic cooperated, he would be with Jenny again at the farmhouse by tea-time.

Smiling, he turned from the railing to face the darkly handsome man standing next to him. "Lovely view from up here."

"Yes," Diego Silvera said, and returned the smile. "A lovely view, Mr. Fanning."

"Comparable ones in the British West Indies, though, I should think. Homes like yours, too. I can't decide between St. Croix and St. Kitts. Have you been to either?"

"No."

"Well. I'm sure I'll like it there. We, I should say. My wife and I. I don't anticipate any problems."

"Nor do I," Silvera said, smiling.

Fanning finished his drink, deciding as he did so that he liked this man, liked his smile and his straightforward manner. Handsome devil, too handsome, but one felt at ease with him, secure in his hands. Oh, everything was progressing nicely. In another few days—

Silvera said, "Do you have the diamonds with you, Mr. Fanning?"

Fanning was startled; he almost dropped his glass. He hadn't said a word to the man about the diamonds. The phrase he'd used was "precious commodity."

"It would be best if I kept them, don't you think?" Silvera said. He was rotating a heavy quartz ring on the third finger of his right hand.

"How . . . how did you know I . . ?"

"I know many things, Mr. Fanning."

"Yes, but—"

"It really would be best if you gave me the diamonds."

"No," Fanning said. "No, I'm sorry, no."

"It would be safer."

"They're quite safe now."

"Then you don't have them with you?"

"No, I do not."

"Where are they?"

"Now really, that's not your concern."

"Ah, but it is."

"Well, I don't agree. Now if you don't mind—"

"Where are they, Mr. Fanning?"

"Listen here," Fanning said, irritated now. "I don't believe I care for your—" and Silvera, still smiling, struck him in the mouth with his right hand, the one that had the quartz ring on the third finger.

The blow sent Fanning staggering backward against the stone barbecue, almost twisting him inside it. The glass he'd been holding sprayed him with ice, slipped free of his fingers and shattered on the floor. Blood ran from a gash across his upper lip.

"The diamonds," Silvera said, still smiling.

Fanning touched his lip as he straightened, looked at the blood shining on his fingertips. He said disbelievingly, "Why? Why did you do that?"

"The diamonds," Silvera said again.

"What kind of man *are* you? I came to you in good faith—"

"The diamonds. Tell me where they are."

"Go to hell!"

Silvera moved quickly without seeming to, struck Fanning again. With the flat of his palm this time, only then he brought the hand back and dragged the quartz ring so that it opened a long bleeding cut in Fanning's cheek. "The diamonds," he said in the same pleasant voice, but he was no longer smiling. His eyes were unnaturally bright. "Where are they? Tell me where they are."

"You bloody bastard!"

Fanning lowered his head and charged the other man, making angry, frightened sounds in his throat. Silvera stepped sideways and cuffed him with the right hand again, knuckles up, the quartz ring gleaming in the sunlight. A jagged flap of skin tore loose under Fanning's chin. He spun away, almost fell, regained his balance by catching hold of the balcony railing. He stood with tears leaking out of his eyes, blood leaking out of the cuts on his face, trembling violently, trying to understand what was happening here, failing because the attack had been so sudden and unprovoked, he had liked this man, trusted him, it had all been going so beautifully . . .

"This is the last time I will ask you, Mr. Fanning," Silvera said. "Where are the diamonds?"

This isn't right, it isn't fair, Fanning thought, you have no right to them, I took them for Jennifer, you have no right! He stumbled forward with a quickness that surprised Silvera, swinging his right hand up blindly, and even though he'd never been in a fight in his life he managed to catch Silvera on the cheekbone, solidly, his knuckles scraping skin away.

The blow unleashed a savage fury in Silvera. He began

hitting Fanning with both hands—broke his nose, made him shriek in pain, kept hitting him and hitting him, harder each time, a look on Silvera's face now of something close to ecstacy, and then another crunching blow that almost tore his ear off, pitched him around and hard against the railing.

Fanning felt his feet go out from under him, his body lift up horizontally; felt himself tilting backward over the railing, Silvera'a hands clawing at him but failing to catch hold; felt himself falling, everything spinning crazily.

His last thought was: It isn't fair I love you Jenny you brought me alive and now—

MONDAY AFTERNOON – JENNIFER

Under the grape arbor in front of the farmhouse, Jennifer Evans sat staring at the pine wood and wondering what was keeping Allen.

She wore a white bikini, and perspiration glistened on the smooth tan of her legs and belly and shoulders. She sat with her legs splayed out in front of her because the sweat had gotten down between her legs and begun to chafe. She wished she had a gin-and-tonic with plenty of ice; but there were no refrigeration facilities at the farm, and no gin and tonic either. If only Allen would hurry up. He'd promised to take her to Puerto Pollensa tonight for a swim and dinner. He was already more than two hours late. Where was he, for heaven's sake?

Jennifer shifted slightly, drawing her legs open wider; the rusted springs of the swing made protesting noises. She was suffocating here, didn't he realize that? He was so damned methodical, that was the trouble. Anyone else would have been able to arrange things quite as well in half the time. Oh come on, Allen, she thought, I'm hungry and I'd like that swim and I want some gin. I mean it, pet, you'd better hurry up.

She shifted again, and the bikini top pinched the skin along her back. Damn! She reached around and unfastened the catch, pulling the cloth away from her breasts. She didn't need to wear the top, there was nobody around to see. It was so bloody *hot*!

And this place . . . God, Allen had plunked them down in the middle of nowhere. This forsaken place was deep in the interior, miles and miles from Palma and civilization, where there were more farm animals than people. Santa Margarita, Alcudia, Arta . . . names that meant nothing, dusty villages no one in his right mind would want to visit, much less live in. The nearest one with a store—she couldn't remember its name—was ten kilometers away, much too far to walk. Even in Puerto Pollensa there was nothing to do except eat awful food and drink gin-and-tonics and have yourself a dip.

Farmland and fig and almond trees, that was all there was to look at around here. And those ancient, crumbling rock walls that ran in all directions, climbing hillocks, disappearing into thick woods. Allen had told her they were constructed by the Moors centuries ago—as if she fucking cared.

She looked at the farmhouse and yard with loathing. The stone-and-mortar house seemed to sag downward in the middle as if it would collapse any minute. It didn't even have a door, just two dozen hanging strands of colored glass beads. Red earth . . . prickly pear cactus . . . a rotting wagon wheel and the remains of the cart it had come from . . . two stone outbuildings, two empty livestock corrals . . . and the well. You not only had to carry water inside in a wooden bucket, you had to work the windlass by hand. There was no electricity, and no indoor plumbing. The loo was an outhouse in back that stunk to high heaven.

Allen had said they'd be safe here, that no one could

possibly find them until they were ready to leave for the Caribbean. Well, he'd certainly been right about that. Not even *God* could find them in a bloody backwater like this.

Abruptly Jennifer stood and went inside the house, where it was even hotter but at least not quite so ugly and depressing to look at. The owners had somewhere found a huge eagle-claw bathtub, and last night Allen had carried in several buckets of water from the well to fill it. The water was still in the tub—warm now, of course, and filmed with the red dust that seemed to cover everything in and out of the house, but at least *wet*. She went back there and took off the bikini briefs and got naked into the tub.

She was a tall woman, with a model's slender figure and a model's clean, calculated movements. Her blond hair, the color and texture of cornsilk, was clipped short, and together with round, wondering eyes, it gave her a young and innocent look. That too was calculated. She was still relatively young, at least in years, but she hadn't been innocent in a long time.

She had had her first sexual encounter at fifteen; and when she'd left school at eighteen she had become the mistress of the owner of a small modeling agency in London. Both men had been in their forties. She had always been attracted to older men. She had never known her father—he had left his family for a Cardiff bar girl when Jennifer was a baby—and her mother had raised her alone, bitterly teaching her the untrustworthiness of men and the folly of love. Teaching her material gain as the key to happiness and security, because they were poor and she didn't want her daughter to live the kind of life of privation that she had.

The owner of the modeling agency had taught her, among other things, the love of fine clothing. But he wasn't wealthy enough to give her all that she wanted, so she'd left him eventually with high hopes. With each passing year, the hopes had diminished. She wasn't beautiful enough, nor educated nor clever enough, to link herself to the one man who could make her happy; she passed from hand to hand among the middle-aged, moderately well-off men of the fashion world, who gave her nothing more than minor material comforts and adequate modeling jobs in exchange for the enjoyment of her slender young body.

She awoke one morning to the realization that she was twenty-seven years old, that there were tiny lines forming under her eyes, and that in another ten years, if she stayed in London under her present circumstances, she would be too old to be either a model or a mistress. The thought terrified her, the more so because it would mean she would one day die alone, bitter and unfulfilled, as her mother had died three years before.

To the surprise of everyone, including herself, she had fled England and come to the Continent. She chose Spain because it was inexpensive, and Málaga because it was known as the Nice of the Spanish Riviera. She went with renewed hopes, but at the end of six months she had slept with four different men ranging in age from forty-six to fifty-eight, from four different countries, and each of them had been like the ones she had known in London—no wealthier, no more successful.

And then she had met Allen.

She was tired then, even more anxious; the last thing she'd wanted was an affair with a man who was even poorer than her usual conquests. But he was so gentle, so kind, so understanding . . . she'd given in in a moment of weakness. A few days later she'd broken it off. He'd begged her, desperately, not to; she'd been adamant. And in a rare moment of candor, she'd told him why.

The next night he'd told her about the diamonds.

She hadn't felt shock or fear or any moral misgivings. Relief, at first, and then gratitude, and then exhiliration. If he did this thing for her, stole for her, would she come with him to some other part of the world, the Caribbean perhaps, and marry him? Oh yes, Allen, she'd said, yes— thinking about what the diamonds would buy, all the gowns and furs and security and happiness that would finally be hers . . .

Lying in the dusty water of the tub, her eyes squeezed tightly shut, Jennifer thought of the diamonds again now. Allen had shown them to her the night he'd taken them — twenty-five cut and polished, blue and yellow diamonds ranging in size from four to ten carats, valued on the open market at something more than two hundred thousand British pounds sterling.

Her fingers tingled at the remembered touch of them. Cool, like ice — like glittering ice. Where had Allen put them? she wondered. He hadn't told her and she hadn't thought to ask. Well, he hadn't taken them with him, she was certain of that. It would have been foolish to carry them around, and Allen was never foolish. They were somewhere close by, here in the house. Not hidden; he wouldn't have hidden them from her. They should be easy to find.

Jennifer lifted herself out of the tub, not bothering to towel herself dry, and padded naked into the bedroom. She would find them, she thought, those beautiful diamonds, and then she would hold their coolness against her body, rub them over her breasts, let the icy feel of them soothe away the heat while she waited for Allen to come back . . .

MONDAY AFTERNOON – CARMODY

The address the Dutch fence, Zaanhof, had given him on the phone surprised Carmody a little when he got there. It was a storefront on a middle-class neighborhood shopping street not far from the Oosterpark. A confectioner's shop with a sign in the front window that said its specialty was *hopjes* coffee candy.

He paid the taxi driver, stood with Gillian on one of the *rijwielpads* that ran alongside the motor lanes on most of Amsterdam's streets: bicycles here outnumbered cars, trucks, and buses. At their backs, a glass-domed tourist boat drifted past on the sunlit Singelgracht Canal and there were people and geese under the sycamores on the canal banks.

Gillian said, "What are we waiting for?"

Carmody didn't answer. He was peering across at the confectioner's shop. After a couple of minutes he said, "You don't know anything about this man Zaanhof?"

"No, I told you, only that Virgil recommended him as being completely trustworthy. Why, what's the matter?"

"Maybe nothing. But hot-diamond merchants don't usually operate out of candy stores in neighborhoods like this one."

"Well, so what?" She toyed nervously with the silver bracelet on her left wrist. "You called somebody about Zaanhof, didn't you?"

"My contact never heard of him."

"That doesn't mean anything, you said so yourself."

"I said it didn't have to mean anything. There's a difference."

"Oh for God's sake, can't we just get this over with? If I'm not worried, why should you be?"

"It's one of the things you're paying me for."

But there wasn't any good reason to hold off. It was true that Van Hagen, his Dutch contact, had never heard of Zaanhof and had been unable to find out anything about him on short notice; and it was true that diamond fences didn't usually work out of neighborhoods or businesses like the ones here. But neither fact was cause for alarm. Van Hagen didn't know everybody operating in the Amsterdam underworld, particularly the small-timers and part-timers; Zaanhof might also be new at the trade, or working under deep cover for reasons of his own. Hell, it was a simple cash-for-merchandise transaction, wasn't it? Why make something sinister out of it?

Just get it done, he thought, and then hustle her back to the Beatrix to wait for Van Hagen's man to deliver her new passport. If he brought it by six tonight, as promised, they'd be on the eight o'clock KLM plane for Dublin. On the flight up from Palma she'd told him she didn't much care where she started her new life; he'd suggested Ireland and she said that was fine. Once he got her safely to Dublin, his job was finished and he could head back to Majorca. With any luck he'd be home two days from now. And shut of Gillian Waltham for good.

Waiting with her at the hotel had been a trial for both

of them. At his insistence they'd left their room only once, to take Sunday dinner in the Beatrix's dining room; he'd had breakfast and lunch sent up both days. They rarely spoke to each other, and Gillian kept well apart from him whenever she could. The whole thing was pretty god-damned silly, as far as he was concerned. She was like a naive young bride pouting after her first big marital row ... an attitude that was in direct contradiction to the diamond run she'd made. He couldn't figure her out and it bothered him. Being close to her, in private like that, bothered him too. In spite of what he'd told her, he wanted her body. She was a damned attractive woman for all her screwy ways ...

"Well?" she said irritably. "Are we going or not?"

"We're going."

Carmody took her arm, steered her across the street. At the door to Zaanhof's shop he said, "I'll do all the talking," and then led her inside.

The place was well-stocked with chocolates and fruit drops and wafers, as well as *hopjes* candy; the combined smells reminded Carmody of a store in the San Francisco neighborhood where he'd grown up. There was nobody behind any of the glass-fronted cases, but a bell had gone off when they entered and it brought a round, pink, smiling little man out through a rear doorway.

"Hello, hello," he said, "welcome."

Carmody said, "Are you Zaanhof?"

"I am."

"I'm Carmody. This is Gillian Waltham."

"A pleasure, *mijnheer.*" He bowed to Gillian; his fat blue eyes caressed her body with approval. "Dear lady, a pleasure."

Gillian said nothing. Now that they were here she seemed nervous, tense.

Zaanhof consulted a platinum watch on one wrist. "Exactly on time. Very good. I admire punctuality."

"Yes? This is some place you've got here."

"Do you like it? I have a great fondness for candies of

all types." He laughed and patted his round belly. "As you no doubt see for yourself."

"You don't dress like a candy butcher."

"Butcher? Ah, you mean seller. Candy seller, yes. It is my assistant who sells the candy, you see. I have sent him away. He is not aware of my other, ah, interests."

Zaanhof laughed again; he liked himself a lot, this Dutchman. He was in his fifties, with a face as smooth and innocent as a baby's and graying hair barbered so short it was like a wool skullcap. Oversized panda bear, Carmody thought, dressed in a dove-gray silk suit, pale yellow shirt, black bow tie. Cool, affluent, convival—the trust-me image. Honorable dishonesty, served up with a smile.

Carmody didn't like him. He hadn't liked the soft oily voice on the telephone, and Zaanhof in person was even less appealing.

"You going to do business out here?" Carmody asked.

"No, no. In my private office."

"Somebody else back there?"

"No one. We are alone here."

"What if a customer comes in?"

"Not to worry," the Dutchman said cheerfully. He went to the front door, locked it, then hung a placard in the window that told passersby the shop was closed. "Shall we, Heer Carmody? Dear lady?"

The office he showed them into was small, dark, cluttered. Zaanhof sat down behind the desk, gestured for them to occupy the room's other two chairs. Gillian took one of them; Carmody remained standing.

"Now then," Zaanhof said. "To business. May I see the diamonds please, dear lady?"

"Yes, certainly," she said and looked at Carmody.

He said to Zaanhof, "Have you got the money?"

"But of course, *mijnheer.*"

"We'll see that first. Then the diamonds."

"As you wish."

Zaanhof opened a bottom drawer, removed a cloth satchel, set the satchel on the desktop, and opened it.

Carmody saw packets of U.S. currency, the top bill on each a hundred. Gillian, too, leaned forward to glance inside. Then she nodded and again looked at Carmody.

"Count it out," he told the Dutchman.

She said with nervous anger, "Damn you, why do you have to make trouble *now*? I'm sure the money's all there."

Carmody wasn't. Any good fence would have had the cash ready in time for his customer's arrival; Zaanhof hadn't even had it yesterday, had made them wait until this afternoon. Things like that made Carmody suspicious. "Well, Zaanhof?"

The Dutchman shrugged and said again, "As you wish."

He got to his feet, so casually and unhurriedly, his attention apparently on the satchel, that the sudden appearance of the gun in his hand took Carmody by surprise. Zaanhof must have had the small-caliber automatic in the desk drawer with the satchel, must have taken it out at the same time. Carmody's hand went reflexively to his belt, even though it was too late by then; but he didn't draw the Beretta. Zaanhof's soft, oily voice stopped him.

"No, no, Mr. Carmody. I wouldn't like to shoot you but I will if you make it necessary. Believe me, I will."

Gillian said, "Oh, God," moaning the words.

Carmody said thinly, "What's the idea, Zaanhof?"

"The idea," the Dutchman told him, "is that the satchel contains quite a bit less than one hundred thousand American dollars. You left me no choice."

"What happens now?"

"First Miss Waltham will remove your weapon and give it to me. Dear lady, if you please."

Gillian was pale, frightened—but there didn't seem to be much surprise in her. Nor any outrage. She got to her feet without looking at Carmody, used two fingers to lift the Beretta out of its holster. She handed the gun to Zaanhof and he made it disappear.

"Does Mr. Carmody have the diamonds or do you?"

"He does."

"Mijnheer, if you please."

Carmody opened the top buttons of his shirt, pulled the chamois pouch over his head. Instead of handing over the pouch, he opened it and spilled the diamonds into his palm. Zaanhof didn't object when he did that, or when he slapped them down on the desktop. The Dutchman scooped the gems up with his free hand, made them disappear too. He didn't seem to notice that there were only four, not five, because Carmody had palmed the fifth. Gillian didn't seem to notice either.

"Behind you, to your left," Zaanhof said then, "is a door. You will turn around, please, open the door, and step inside."

Carmody didn't move. "You know who I am, Zaanhof?"

"Naturally."

"Then you also know my reputation. Nobody double-crosses me and gets away with it. Nobody. If you know what's good for you, you'll put that gun away and start apologizing before it's too late."

"Or use it on you, eh? Another alternative?"

"Or use it on me," Carmody said. "One or the other. If you lock me up and walk out of here with the money and the diamonds, you're going to have to worry about me for the rest of your life. I won't be far behind you no matter where you go, and when I find you—and I will, sooner or later—you'll be one sorry son of a bitch."

Gillian made another moaning sound. But Zaanhof only shrugged. "The door behind you, Mr. Carmody. Now."

The door opened on a supply closet not much larger than a coffin and so cluttered there was barely enough room for Carmody to squeeze inside. The door was made of heavy wood. The latch was the old-fashioned kind that locked with a key; the key was in it.

Zaanhof told Gillian to shut and lock the door. She came over and took hold of it, again without meeting Carmody's eyes. In a voice so low he could barely hear her she said, "I'm sorry." And then she shut him into darkness.

It took Carmody more than an hour to get out of the closet. He'd have been in there a lot longer than that—he couldn't get enough leverage in the cramped space to kick or batter the door down with his shoulder—if he hadn't had his Swiss Army knife with him. At that, working blind in the dark, gouging out wood on the door and jamb so he could reach the latch bolt, he was lucky to escape as fast as he did.

Zaanhof and the woman were long gone. Streaming sweat, Carmody quick-searched the office and the rest of the shop. He found nothing that gave him a lead to where Zaanhof lived or might have gone—if Zaanhof was the Dutchman's real name, which wasn't likely. One thing was certain: he didn't own this confectioner's shop. The owner was a man named Hubert TenEyck; there were papers to that effect in the desk.

Carmody had to walk all the way to Utrectsestraat before he found one of the black Mercedes diesels that served as Amsterdam's taxis. When he walked into the Beatrix twenty minutes later, the concierge was away from his desk. Carmody reached around and plucked the key to his room out of its slot. He rode the elevator upstairs.

His suitcase was sitting where he'd left it. The two belonging to Gillian Waltham were gone.

Carmody cursed softly. Then he lifted the phone, jiggled the cradle until the concierge came on. "The girl I was with," he said, "what time did she check out?"

"About forty minutes ago, sir. She said you would be joining her later."

"Was anybody with her?"

"An older gentleman."

"Short, chubby, wearing a gray silk suit?"

"Yes, sir."

"They give you any idea where they were going?"

"No, I'm afraid not. Is it important, sir?"

"It will be to them when I find them."

He called Van Hagen, told him what had happened. Gave him Hubert TenEyck's name and the address of the candy shop—the only leads he had to Zaanhof's true identity. Then he rang up room service, ordered a bottle of Napoleon cognac. He was sipping cognac and smoking a cigar when Van Hagen arrived a half hour later.

Van Hagen was a thin, sad-eyed man in rumpled clothing. In addition to being a contact man and a black marketeer, he had a certain amount of expertise with diamonds. Carmody gave him the stone he'd palmed. Van Hagen looked at it through a loupe, then shook his head dourly.

"Synthetic," he said. "Of good quality but worth very little."

Carmody threw his cognac glass against the wall, watched it shatter with eyes that shone like green fire.

MONDAY AFTERNOON — SILVERA

In the pines at the foot of the steep fall, Silvera had begun digging a shallow grave. Nearby, what was left of Allen Fanning lay broken and bloodied and host to a swarm of hungry flies.

Silvera worked rapidly, in a thin anger that made his temples pound. Damn Fanning and the man's foolish stubbornness! But the fault was as much his; if he had taken his time, exercised more control over his impatience and his passion, Fanning would have eventually told him where the diamonds were. *Then* he could have beaten the Britisher to death, slowly, slowly. As it was he had no idea where to find the diamonds, except that it was probable they were in the possession of the woman he had referred to as his wife. Fanning had carried no papers that revealed his hiding place on the island or his woman's name. One small clue . . . that was all Silvera had to go on.

When he finished digging he slashed at the buzzing

flies with the shovel, then used his foot to roll the dead man into the shallow grave. He scraped dirt over the body, patted the loose earth down. It was not the most concealing of burial places; but it would not be visible from the villa's balcony or patio.

He climbed up the slope to the patio wall, then onto the balcony. There was blood and broken glass on the floor. Inside, he filled an earthenware *olla* with water, found a handful of paper towels and a plastic grocery sack. He swept the broken glass into the bag, cleaned up the spots of blood, put the paper towels in with the shards, returned the *olla* to the kitchen. Then he examined the balcony again: no signs of the fight remained. The diamonds were of paramount importance, to be sure, but the *patrón* did not like loose ends and the *patrón* would be displeased enough if the diamonds were not found quickly.

He relocked the balcony doors, climbed down to the patio, crossed to the parking area in front. Fanning's rental car, a Seat 600, sat next to the 1200 he had rented. Silvera drove the 1200 down the winding access road to a spot where he could pull off into the pines. He took out his leather carry-all, transferred the Browning automatic into it from his belt, threw the plastic grocery bag into the trees, then hurried back to the clearing.

He deposited his carry-all in the trunk of Fanning's 600. A rapid search of the car yielded nothing but a map of the island, unmarked. But the 600 was still his one lead to the whereabouts of the diamonds. The keys, which he had taken from Fanning's pocket, were inside a leather case that had the name of a Palma rental agency stamped on it. Silvera knew that in order to rent a car on the island, Fanning would have had to provide a local address. He also knew that there was nothing to have prevented Fanning from giving a false address, but he would not worry about that possibility now.

He drove the 600 Seat away from there, back to Palma.

The heavy-breasted young woman behind the counter

in the rental office was more than a little flustered by his dazzling smile. But she was also afraid to bend strict agency rules. "I would like to help you, *señor,* I truly would. You understand?"

"I understand," Silvera said, smiling, stroking her with his eyes, "and I would not ask except for this." He showed her Fanning's billfold, opening it to an identification card in one of the celluloid windows. "It slipped from the man's pocket as he was getting into his rental car in El Terreno half an hour ago. I called after him but he did not hear or see me. There is nothing in the wallet to lead me to him. I have only the name of your agency."

"Why don't you take the wallet to the Guardia Civil?" she asked. "They will hold it until the owner can be found."

"Undoubtedly. And undoubtedly you would perform the same service if I were to leave it with you. However, I would prefer to give the wallet to Señor Fanning myself."

"But why?"

Another of his smiles, a small wink, a shrug. "Perhaps he might find it in his heart to offer a small reward. It would not be too much to ask, *verdad?*"

"You seem much too well-dressed to be thinking of rewards, *señor.*"

"Appearances deceive. You would not begrudge a poor but honest man a few extra pesetas, surely? Not a girl as lovely and understanding as yourself."

She giggled. "Perhaps," she said, "I could make an exception this one time, in such a good cause."

"I would be forever in your debt."

"Oh, would you? And how would you repay this debt?"

Coño estupido! Silvera thought. But his outwardly relaxed pose remained fixed; he forced more intimacy into his smile. "With an evening of dancing in El Terreno. And if the Señor Fanning does see fit to reward me, a fine dinner as well."

"I would like that," the girl said. "Tonight?"

"Tonight, yes."

"I am finished here at seven."

"*Querida,* I will count the minutes."

Another giggle, moist eyes bright. "My name is Carmine," she said. "Carmine Ortega. And yours?"

"Carlos," Silvera said. "Carlos Vargas."

"Where will we dance, Carlos? The J&B?"

Coño, coño, puta! An urge rose inside him, tingling; he wanted to reach across the counter and slap her silly face, wrap his hands tightly around her soft, pulsing throat . . .

"The J&B, and then Barbarella's."

"Barbarella's!"

"The *señor's* address now? I have much to do, and I must go quickly if I am to be back here at seven."

The girl stood, smoothed her suede mini-skirt over plump thighs. "You must never tell that I do this for you, Carlos."

"Never. No, never."

"The license number again?"

He gave her the slip of paper on which he had written the number. She crossed to a bank of filing cabinets, teasing him with her hips. Silvera did not even look at her; she was a mound of clay to him. She fussed in one of the drawers, removed a folder, opened it, read a typed form. When she came back to him he brightened his smile again, fixed his eyes on her breasts.

But she was pouting now. "The Seat was rented by a woman," she said. "A Miss Jennifer Evans."

"A friend of Señor Fanning's, perhaps. His lover, perhaps."

"Not one you wish to make *your* lover, Carlos?"

"You doubt me, *querida?*"

"Well . . ."

"I have no interest in any woman at this moment but Carmine Ortega."

Desire chased away her doubts; her pout disintegrated. "The Evans woman's address is the Hotel Mediterráneo."

"*Gracias, querida.* If Señor Fanning is not there, the Señorita Evans will know where to reach him."

"You will not forget to come at seven, Carlos?"

"I will not forget," Silvera lied.

He drove quickly to the Hotel Mediterráneo. It was one of the new high-rise luxury hotels on the Paseo Maritimo, constructed of white stone and imitation marble, with jutting pastel balconies that overlooked the harbor of Palma. Inside, Silvera approached the concierge, asked for the room number of Señorita Jennifer Evans. An urgent matter concerning her rental car, he said.

The concierge consulted a guest list. "I am sorry, *señor*, we have no one registered by that name."

"You are sure?"

"Quite sure, *señor*."

"A Britisher named Fanning, then? Allen Fanning?"

Another consultation with the list. And another headshake. "No *señor*. No one by that name either."

Silvera's headache had returned. He entered the hotel bar, ordered a Scotch, drank it neat, and called for a second. So Fanning's woman was named Jennifer Evans. She had given a false address, but she would have had to show her passport at the rental agency; the name was her real one. But where was she? How could he find her? Jennifer Evans . . . another Britisher. And there were thousands of Britishers on Majorca, in hotels and bungalows and villas. How would he find her?

Yes, and what would he tell the *patrón?*

MONDAY,
LATE AFTERNOON — JENNIFER

She could not find the diamonds.

She had searched the farmhouse thoroughly—bedroom, parlor, kitchen, pantry, rear porch, Allen's luggage, her own luggage, everywhere—and now she stood again by the tub of dusty and tepid water trying to understand. Had he taken the diamonds with him after all? And where *was* he, for God's sake? He had been gone nearly eight hours now.

Absently, she rubbed perspiration from her bare breasts. Something was wrong. And yet she couldn't quite make herself believe it. Allen had told her the man he was seeing was completely trustworthy, but if he'd taken the diamonds with him and shown them to this man . . . no, he wouldn't do that, he wouldn't. He had told her he was leaving them here, she remembered that now, and he would never lie to her. Not Allen.

Perhaps he's had an accident, she thought, some kind

of accident with the car. The only other explanation she could think of was that he'd been found somehow by the ones who worked for the man Allen had stolen the diamonds from. If that was it, they would make him tell about the farmhouse and then they would come here and torture her and maybe kill her . . . oh, that was daft, how *could* they have found Allen? He had been so careful, they couldn't know about the man he was seeing or even that he had come to Majorca.

Then where was he?

And where were those lovely fucking diamonds?

Jennifer felt panic stirring inside her, struggled to get a grip on herself. Perhaps she was overreacting; perhaps Allen was still being bloody methodical in arranging things and he would return soon and the diamonds . . . the diamonds *must* still be here, she had simply missed them somehow in her search.

She began to feel a little better, calm again. She drank a glass of warm well water, made a face at the acrid mineral taste, and then went into the dark and humid parlor to look outside. The rocky entry road and the red-earth farmyard shimmered with heat mirage, and the pines stood absolutely motionless, like backdrops on a stage set. In the sky overhead, a hawk wheeled in slow motion—drifting lower and lower with each turn, hunting prey. The silence had a hollow quality to it, brittle and breathless.

Out there? she thought then. Would he have put the diamonds outside somewhere?

She pushed through the glass beads, walked along the side of the house and under the arbor, pausing at each of the pieces of homemade furniture and at the deteriorating metal swing. Over by the stone well, then, and the outbuildings, and the corrals. Looking, looking, finding nothing.

Sweat coated her, burned in the grotto of her thighs. The urgency was growing in her again; she felt the panic again. She ran back to the house and searched the bedroom another time, their luggage, each of the other rooms.

 No diamonds, no diamonds, no diamonds . . .

MONDAY EVENING – GILLIAN

The man who was calling himself Peter Zaanhof lived in a white stone villa on the western outskirts of Málaga, set into the low foothills a half mile from the sea. Mauve-colored bougainvillea, thick and fragrant, clung to the whole of the wide facing wall, and there were tall palm trees in the front yard. It was all very nice, especially with the sky aflame with sunset colors and the Mediterranean like burning phosphorous in the distance, but Gillian didn't want to be here. She didn't like Zaanhof, for one thing. And for another, she was still afraid. Of Carmody mostly— that he would find her before she could get out of Spain, and of what he would do to her if he did.

The taxi driver removed their luggage from the trunk, and Zaanhof paid him; a moment later Gillian stood alone with the Dutchman in the gathering twilight. He said, "Do you find it appealing, dear lady?"

"Your villa? Yes, it's beautiful. But I still wish you'd paid me in Amsterdam. Or at the airport here."

Zaanhof smiled. "But dear lady, I have already explained and apologized. There were so many arrangements to make, here and in Amsterdam—"

"Yes, all right. It doesn't matter as long as you pay me now."

"But of course. Did you doubt that I would?"

"No. No, I never doubted it." But she had, and still did, and would until she had the money in her hands.

Zaanhoff tried to pat or stroke her arm; she avoided the contact. He shrugged and smiled at her again in that moist, treacley way of his. It made her nervous because she knew now what lay behind it, the duplicity and the capacity for violence that he had demonstrated in the candy shop in Amsterdam.

She hadn't bargained for that scene with the gun, the doublecross against Carmody. God, she'd almost wet herself. Zaanhof had told her in the beginning that there would be no trouble, that it was all an elaborate but harmless ruse. Well, it wasn't harmless at all. She had known that after spending five minutes with Carmody; nothing that man was involved in was harmless. But she had committed herself by then, and the lure of the two thousand dollars Zaanhof had promised her was too strong for her to try to back out. She *would* have backed out, though, if she'd known what was going to happen in the candy store. And if she'd known the truth about the diamonds.

Zaanhof had told her about the diamonds while they were on the way to the Beatrix to pick up her bags. That the stones weren't real. He'd led her to believe they were, he said, because it would be easier for her to convince Carmody if she believed it herself. He hadn't been concerned about what Carmody would say or do when *he* found out they weren't real. Carmody's threat didn't seem to bother him, either. It was a pity he'd had to close the transaction by gunpoint, he said, but Carmody's insistence on counting the money had made it necessary. There had been only ten thousand dollars in the satchel. He hadn't been able to raise any more cash on such short notice. She thought that was a lie, too, but it didn't make any difference, really. It was a *fait accompli* either way.

None of the game-playing made much sense to her. At first she had hoped to find out what it was all about, but after two days in the hotel room with Carmody—and especially now—she didn't want to know. All she wanted was her money, a good night's sleep in a *pension* in Málaga, a seat on a plane out of Spain tomorrow, and another seat on a plane home to the States on Wednesday.

Zaanhof picked up her bags, and his own, and led her through the lush garden. Inside the villa it was dark and considerably cooler. The furnishings were Old Spanish, heavily scrolled, with rococo brass ornamentation. None of it looked very comfortable, including the long couch upholstered in tapestried cloth that he invited her to sit on. She remained standing in the middle of the room, on one of several braided rugs opposite a deep stone fireplace. There were olive-wood statuettes on the fireplace mantel, intricately carved, of different kinds of animals; she looked at them to keep from looking at Zaanhof.

"If you don't mind, Mr. Zaanhof," she said, "I'd like to keep the rest of our business as brief as possible."

"Won't you call me Peter?"

"My money . . . Peter. Please."

"Of course, dear lady. But first, a drink."

"I don't care for one, thanks."

"Ah, but we have had a long day. A drink will refresh you."

"Thank you, but—"

"Dry Sack, perhaps? Do you like sherry?"

"Yes, but I really don't—"

"Excellent," Zaanhof said, and before she could protest again he turned quickly and left the room.

Gillian sighed, sank wearily onto the couch. Well, all right, she would have one glass of sherry. It would do her no good to offend the Dutchman now, and she was too exhausted to argue anyway.

She closed her eyes, thinking of home—Canton, the house she had grown up in, her mother and father. Almost a year, now, since she'd taken the money she'd carefully saved over five years of part-time jobs and come to Europe to pursue her acting career. She could hardly believe what an innocent girl she had been when she'd left the States, how immature for a twenty-three-year-old college graduate. All starry-eyed and full of plans, convinced that the Italian and French film directors who spent their summers in Biarritz and Cannes and Nice would notice her, be impressed by her talent, give her the kind of entré into the film world that she could never get in the Hollywood jungle. Attractive and talented American girls were always very much in demand in the foreign market, weren't they?

Yes, they were, but the market they were in demand for had nothing to do with films.

The predators, hungry and waiting, almost devoured her in the first month.

But she was bright and self-protective and she learned quickly. She learned that pretty girls with a desire to become actresses, even those with more than a little talent, were ten francs a hundred; that the ones with the lushest bodies and the penchant for sexual deviation and promiscuity were the most likely to succeed; that the world of glamour and glitter she had created in her mind was only an illusion, no more genuine than the illusions that world itself created. She'd made a few compromises, but only in the beginning, only until she learned all of her lessons well and grew from a foolish girl into a disenchanted woman. Then she'd packed her bags and fled the predators, gone to Spain to lick her wounds.

A month after her arrival in Málaga, at a sidewalk cafe, handsome, clever Fernando Marí had come into her life. And for a while the new-found cynicism had evaporated, her faith in life and her goals had been restored. She gave herself fully to Fernando for six long, giddy weeks, with the unshakable certainty that she loved him and he loved her in return . . . until the night he had kissed her gently and said, "Goodbye, *querida*," and walked out of her life without looking back. That had been the final disillusionment. And with it had come a revulsion for Europe and all that had happened to her here. *Now* she really was a grown woman, and she knew the time had come for her to quit wasting any more of her life on foolish childhood dreams, to go home and get a job and confine her acting to little theater groups and try to find a much more attainable brand of fulfillment.

The problem was, she was out of money by then. And she dreaded the idea of having to ask her parents for return fare; the inability to get home on her own would have robbed her of what remained of her pride. When Zaanhof had approached her with his offer, he had seemed so much like a godsend that she'd asked few questions and accepted almost immediately . . .

Zaanhof came back into the room with two tulip glasses of sherry. He had taken off his suit coat, opened his shirt at the throat, and he was still smiling, always so damned cheerful. He looked cherubic and grandfatherly. But when he gave her one of the glasses, he also sat down beside her—close beside her, much too close.

"To you, dear lady," he said, raising his glass. "A pleasant trip and future happiness."

"Thank you," Gillian said. She tasted her sherry, then drained the glass too quickly. "Now if you don't mind, I'd like to have my money . . ."

"You are in a rush to leave?"

"I thought I made that clear. I'm very tired."

He watched her eyes. There was a new intensity in his gaze, a kind of deep burning. And all at once Gillian was as frightened of him as she was of Carmody. She started to rise, to put distance between them—and he reached out casually with his free hand and closed his fingers over the soft flesh of her thigh.

Gillian stiffened. "Don't do that," she said. "Let go of me."

Instead he tightened his grip, moved closer. His gaze

was feverish now, his lips moist; there was no mistaking the look of him. She tried to slide sideways, to get up, but his fingers dug painfully into her thigh.

"Stop that! Let me up . . ."

"There is no hurry, dear lady. No hurry at all."

"Damn you, let me go!"

"Fire and ice," Zaanhof murmured. "Fire and ice."

Gillian raked her nails across the back of his hand. He cried out, released his hold; blood welled up along the furrows she'd made. She jumped to her feet and backed away toward the fireplace, thinking that she should have known, men like him were all alike, ugly men, dangerous men, predators . . . she should have known!

He was on his feet too, now, watching her. "Fire and ice," he said.

"No," Gillian said. Firm, direct, without showing fear. Never show fear, they fed on fear. "Don't come any closer, Mr. Zaanhof, I mean it. Just give me my money and let me go, you made a bargain—"

"And I intend to keep it. You shall have your money, dear lady. I ask only your affection in return. Is that too great a request? I am a gentle lover, I will not hurt you, I will only please you. Many men have pleased you, have they not?"

"No!"

Zaanhof's smile was loose, wetly sexual. "A few minutes of passion and we will part friends. I will be generous too, dear lady. An extra five hundred dollars, perhaps an extra thousand—"

"No! What do you think I am?"

His eyes told her what he thought she was. He took two steps toward her, caressing her body with those dirty eyes. She backed away, kept backing until the wall of the fireplace stopped her . . . and then Zaanhof pounced. Put his hands on her, gathered her against his soft, round body, kissed her neck, ground his hips against her in the motions of love.

She struggled frantically, tried to bite him, tried to knee

him. He held her too tightly, pressed hard against the stone wall, his hips pumping at a faster rhythm. She could feel his arousal, and when she moaned deep in her throat he misinterpreted the sound and made the mistake of releasing one of her arms so he could fondle her breast.

Gillian used her nails on him again, this time tearing them along his neck. Zaanhof groaned, but he didn't let go of her; the groan was almost one of pleasure. Her free hand clawed over the stones, struck the mantelpiece, touched one of the heavy wood statuettes. Her fingers closed over it, hefted it, and without thinking she brought it slashing down against his head.

He grunted, released her. Sagged backward and fell to one knee, pawing at the spot where she'd hit him. She tried to get around him, to run, but she hadn't hurt him badly and she wasn't quick enough. He lunged upright and now there was more than lust in his face, there was pain and a terrible, deadly rage; then he lunged at her. She swung at him again with the statuette, blindly, a sidearm swing that missed his head but connected with the side of his neck. She hit him a third time, in the face, heard him yell with pain, saw him stumble as his feet tangled in one of the braided rugs. He toppled over backward, arms flailing. His buttocks struck the floor and then his head collided with a corner on the low table in front of the couch.

Zaanhof's eyes seemed to pop from their sockets. His body stiffened, as if with an electrical shock; then the eyes filmed and the body relaxed and he seemed to shrink within his clothing, like a snail dissolving after you'd poured salt on it. He didn't move.

Gillian dropped the statuette, stared down at him in horror. He was dead. There was blood now, around his head, not much, a little blood, but he was dead . . . those staring eyes, there was no mistake. He was dead.

I killed him, she thought.

Panic ripped at her. And she ran.

MONDAY, MIDNIGHT — CARMODY

When no one came to the door the third time Carmody rang the bell, he went to work on the latch with his Swiss knife.

Calle Salvador Anglada was dark and empty behind him. Middle-class residential neighborhoods like this one, not far from Barcelona's Plaza Toros Arenas bullfight stadium, shut down early. There were thick shadows here in the entranceway of number 52, and he worked with a minimum of noise; he didn't have to worry about being seen. But he was wary just the same.

It took him five minutes to get the door open. Inside was a foyer and a staircase lifting upward into blackness. Carmody shut the door, drew the Beretta, crossed to the stairs. Halfway up, he paused to listen. The house had the feel and stillness of desertion.

He went up the rest of the way, along a short hallway and into a sparsely furnished parlor. He took a slow turn around the parlor, using his pencil flash to guide him. Then he went back into the hallway and checked the other rooms upstairs. They too were deserted.

Carmody holstered the Beretta, reentered the parlor. A rolltop desk, closed but unlocked, stood against the near wall. He sat down in front of it, rolled up the slatted cover, sifted through the papers in drawers and cubbyholes. They were all in Spanish, but he could speak and read the language passably well, as long as he wasn't confronted with the Mallorquina or Catalan dialects. The papers were bills, receipts, a couple of fairly torrid love notes, some miscellaneous personal documents. Nothing for him in any of them.

He closed the desk, went down to the master bedroom. A sliding closet door was open on one side of the room; on the floor inside, thrown there or dropped in haste from the hangers, were scattered items of clothing. Two drawers in a carved-wood dresser were pulled out and empty.

Carmody looked through the nightstands; nothing. He left the bedroom and entered the kitchen. Nothing. In the spare bedroom, in the storage closet, on the rear porch — nothing.

He returned to the landing at the top of the stairs. So José Alvarez had disappeared along with Zaanhof and the girl — and in a hurry. Ordinarily, whenever Alvarez quit Barcelona on business or pleasure, he left word at a mid-city disco bar called El Halcón Negro; but Carmody had gone there from the airport, and no one at El Halcón Negro had seen or heard from Alvarez in days. Carmody hadn't had much doubt that the Spaniard was mixed up in whatever the hell was going on. Now he had gone.

Alvarez's involvement meant big money and important people were also involved. Otherwise he wouldn't have had the guts to jeopardize his operation in Barcelona, his relationship with Carmody. Zaanhof? Possible but not likely. When you're important enough and moneyed enough, you hire things done instead of doing them yourself.

The Dutchman and Gillian Waltham and José Alvarez. And how many others? And who was behind it all, and why?

He went down the stairs, out along Calle Salvador Anglada to where he'd parked his rental car. It was too late to accomplish anything else tonight; and he needed sleep. He drove uptown to Avenida del Generalissimo Franco, took a room at the Hotel de Santander, left a call for seven a.m., and went to bed.

TUESDAY MORNING – CARMODY

As far as Carmody was concerned, Málaga was the asshole of Spain.

Scorched and wilted by the perpetual heat, filled with too many cars and too few transient accommodations and narrow, refuse-littered streets, it still had some inexplicable lure for the tourists. They came in droves, packed the sidewalks and sidewalk cafes, wandered out into busy streets and were picked off at the rate of a hundred a year by hurtling taxis and buses and private cars. Málaga was noisy from dawn to dusk, dusk to dawn. And overpriced. And inhabited by hordes of small-time grifters and con artists who were so afraid of the Guardia Civil that they confined their activities to the pettiest of larcenies— human mosquitoes feeding on little drops of tourist blood. And when the hot winds blew, as they did often enough, Málaga became an oven that cooked your temper and fried your brain. Every time Carmody came here he developed a malignant headache.

He drove in from the airport at ten-thirty, in another rented Mercedes, cursing the reckless Spanish drivers and the witless jaywalking tourists. He had the windows rolled up and the air conditioning on, shutting out the heat and the noise. But already his head was starting to ache.

Before leaving the Hotel de Santander in Barcelona, he had made three calls. The first was to Van Hagen in Amsterdam, but Van Hagen didn't have much to tell him. He hadn't been able to find out anything about the man who'd called himself Zaanhof; no one in the city knew him or could identify him from his description. No one except Hubert TenEyck, and he was of no help at all. Zaanhof had approached him last Saturday, offered him the equivalent of five hundred dollars for one afternoon's use of his candy shop, cash in advance, no questions asked or answered. TenEyck needed the money, a fact that Zaanhof had seemed to know; he'd agreed on the spot. He had never seen Zaanhof before or since, knew nothing about him.

Carmody's other calls had been to his contacts in Madrid and Lisbon. They hadn't had anything for him either. Gillian Waltham was as elusive a figure as Zaanhof —probably a pawn, as young and naive as she was, but she still had some of the answers. And no one named Virgil Franklin lived in Málaga or had any connection with José Alvarez past or present, in Spain or in Portugal. Carmody told both contacts to put the word out on Alvarez, that he wanted him found and held, and gave the American Express office as his Málaga contact address.

He entered the city on Málaga's version of an Avenida del Generalissimo Franco, found street parking, paid ten pesetas to one of the flock of old, gray-uniformed "attendants"; parking was supposed to be free, but if you forgot or refused to pay one of the old men, your car had a way of being ticketed or even towed away. Another example of the cheap grifting that went on here. The dry, hot air was harsh in his lungs as he walked under drooping palms and shade trees to the Plaza del General Quiepo de Llano.

He had to go into three different bookstalls before he found one that had a street map. On the *guia turistica* he located Calle Cristóbal Ortiz, saw that it was just off the Plaza Obispo, not far from where he was now. He found his way there through a maze of narrow, crowded sidestreets.

The Bar Emperador was larger but otherwise no different from the dozens of other open-air bars that littered Málaga and the other resort areas of Spain. Cream pastries displayed without cover for tourists and flies, standard menu of drinks and sandwiches and seafood and strawberries-and-cream; painted on walls and window glass in several languages, tawdry arrangement of tables and chairs all but blocking the cobblestoned passage in front. Two elderly Spaniards sat drinking San Miguel at one of the tables; at another three red-faced British women made dull remarks over chocolate-milk-and-cognac abominations called *lumumbas*. A young waiter in a black suit and a limp bow tie lounged sleepily in the entranceway.

Carmody sat down away from the other customers, ordered a cold San Miguel from the waiter. On the table was a souvenir menu card like the one he'd found in Gillian's purse in Amsterdam. If she lived in Málaga, or was staying in the area, the chances were good that she had come here from Amsterdam. The chances were less good that she was well-enough known at the Bar Emperador for him to pry loose her address, but the bar was one of only two leads he had to her.

When the waiter brought his San Miguel, Carmody asked him in Spanish if he knew a girl named Gillian Waltham, an American girl. Then he described her. As used to tourists as he was, the waiter was a little surprised to hear an American speaking anything but English; it served to make him friendly. No, *señor*, he did not know a girl by that name or description. So many young women, so many Americans, came to the Bar Emperador that it was impossible to know but a few regular customers and she was not among them.

Carmody gave him a hundred-peseta note, asked him to check with the other employees. The San Miguel was cold enough to suit his taste; he drank half of it from the bottle, then lit a cigar and spread open the *guia turistica*. Calle Villalonga, where the Liana Butler listed in Gillian's address book lived, was off the Paseo de la Farola, down near the harbor—a good distance away. He debated walking back to his rental car, decided to hell with fighting the tourists and the traffic. He'd take a taxi instead.

The waiter came back with his head shaking and his hands spread apologetically. Carmody gave him another hundred pesetas, finished his beer, and went hunting a cab.

The building in which Liane Butler lived was a twelve-story apartment complex facing the harbor—one of the cheaply and hurriedly put up brick-and-stucco jobs that the Spaniards favored. There was little or no steel in any of them and they looked as though a stiff breeze would topple them like towers made of kids' building blocks. This one was a year or two old, which meant that it had another three or four before the plumbing and the exposed electrical wiring began to malfunction, and cracks appeared in floors and walls, and it ceased being acceptable to the transplants from other countries and became cheap housing for the natives.

A bank of name-marked mailboxes told him that the Butler woman lived on the sixth floor, rear. Inside, a shuddering elevator took him up to a passageway no wider than a sidewalk. On its left were the apartment entrances, on the right a low wall and a sheer drop into a center courtyard. It was like stepping out onto a parapet.

Carmody stopped before a blue door with Liane Butler's name in a tarnished metal plate at eye level. He rang the bell. There were steps inside, and a chain rattled, and the door opened jerkily; a face framed by long black hair appeared, saying, "Liane, did you forget your key—" And then yellow-brown cat's eyes popped wide, and the door was flung hard toward his face. Carmody hit it with his shoulder, shoved roughly inside.

Just like that he had found Gillian Waltham.

TUESDAY,
LATE MORNING — CARMODY

She backpedaled rapidly into a room adorned with bullfight posters, one hand up to her mouth and her eyes full of trapped terror. Carmody threw the door shut, slid the chain lock into place, took the Beretta off his hip — watching Gillian reach a pair of open glass doors at the far end of the room. She stopped there, looked out onto the balcony, looked back at him and saw the gun. Her face went as white as custard.

"No," she said, "oh God, no!"

"Shut up," Carmody told her. "I'm not going to use this as long as you keep your head and don't give me any trouble. All I want from you are answers. And Zaanhof."

She shook her head — a gesture without meaning. Her cheeks and mouth were puffy with fatigue; for whatever reason, she hadn't slept much last night.

"How . . . how did you find —"

"How do you think?"

Another headshake.

Carmody said, "You the only one here?"

"Yes."

"But you expect Liane?"

"I . . . yes, she went shopping, she should be back . . ."

"What is she to you?"

"A friend . . . just a friend."

"Does she know about me, about Zaanhof?"

"No. No, I didn't tell her anything."

"All right. If she comes while we're talking, you send her away. Make up a story—and don't give her the idea that there's anything wrong."

"I . . . I won't."

"Fine. Now where's Zaanhof?"

Words seemed to clog in her throat. Her lower jaw began to tremble; then her eyes filled and spilled over.

Carmody put the Beretta away. He said tonelessly, "Tears don't work on me, sweetheart. I want answers and I want them straight and fast, without any crap. Where's Zaanhof?"

She coughed, swallowed, got the words unstuck. "I . . . don't know. I don't know where he is."

"The two of you went where from Amsterdam?"

"Here. Málaga."

"Then what?"

"He left me at the airport. And I came . . . straight here. I had a place of my own but I gave it up last week. I was . . . I am going home to the States—"

"Yes? Does Zaanhof live in Málaga?"

"I don't know."

"What's his real name?"

"I don't know."

"You're lying."

"No, I swear, the only name I know him by is Zaanhof."

"What does he do for a living?"

"I don't know."

"Who paid him to set me up with those fake diamonds?"

"I don't know."

"What's behind it all? Why did he want you to keep me occupied for two days in Amsterdam?"

"It was only supposed to be one day."

"Why did it turn out to be two?"

"Zaanhof didn't tell me why."

"The purpose," Carmody said. "What was it?"

"I don't know."

"Bullshit."

"It's the truth!"

"Is it? You don't know anything about Zaanhof, who he is or who he works for, but you helped him set up this whole phony deal. Explain that."

"The money . . . he offered me money . . ."

"How much money?"

"Two thousand dollars. He knew I needed the money to get home, I ran out of money and I . . . it seemed like such a simple thing . . . he knew I'd had acting experience too, that I'd been in the south of France trying to get into foreign films . . ."

There was a rising inflection in her voice, the stirrings of hysteria. Carmody went over and caught her arm and shook her a little, but that only added to her fright. She cringed away from him, as if she thought he was going to start beating on her. He released her arm, backed up a couple of paces.

"Calm down, I'm not going to hurt you." He gave her time to realize that he meant it, to get her breathing and her emotions under control. Then he said, "Nice and slow now. How did Zaanhof know you needed money, that you're an actress?"

"He said he'd . . . he'd heard about me from a mutual friend."

"What mutual friend?"

"He wouldn't say. He insisted it didn't matter."

Carmody said, "So Zaanhof offered you two thousand dollars to play a part. That's all?"

"Yes."

"When did he make the offer?"

"Last week . . . Thursday."

"What did he tell you it was all about?"

"A harmless ruse, he said. It wouldn't be dangerous and there wouldn't be any trouble."

"He gave you all your lines, told you exactly what to do?"

"Everything, yes. We rehearsed it several times to be sure I knew what to say, and he changed some things; he said you'd ask a lot of questions and the story had to be convincing. When you went through my things in the hotel and found out I hadn't come from Spain I just . . . I ad-libbed about the industrialist being Spanish instead of French."

"Who made up Virgil Franklin, Zaanhof or you?"

"He did."

"José Alvarez is real," Carmody said.

"Yes, Zaanhof told me he was."

"But you don't know him?"

"No. I've never even been to Barcelona."

"Talk to him? Or did Zaanhof make all the arrangements with Alvarez?"

"Zaanhof did."

"He give you the diamonds too?"

Gillian nodded. "Just before I left for Majorca. I gave him one of my bras the night before and he had them sewn into it. I never saw the diamonds until you cut them out in Amsterdam."

"He tell you they were imitations?"

"Only after we left you in that candy shop. I believed they were real before that—he wanted me to believe they were real so I'd be more convincing with you. That's why I didn't want you to keep them, why I . . . made a fuss. I didn't want to be held responsible if anything happened to them."

"Did you know he was going to pull a gun on me in the shop? Lock me in the closet?"

"No! That wasn't part of the script."

"What was supposed to happen?"

"He'd give us the money in exchange for the diamonds and we'd leave. Then I was supposed to slip away from you at the airport, with the money, and return it to him later on."

"Why didn't he work it that way?"

"He said he couldn't raise a hundred thousand dollars and he had no choice. But I didn't believe him. I think the real reason is that he didn't trust me to return the money to him."

"He should have trusted you," Carmody said. "And he should have believed me when I told him he was going to be a sorry son of a bitch."

"He didn't seem worried about you at all," Gillian said.

"That's his second mistake."

Carmody was satisfied that she had no idea why the Dutchman and whoever he was working for had gone to such elaborate measures. She was a pawn, all right—young and foolish and gullible. Zaanhof was the one with the answers. It was Zaanhof he had to find, and the way it looked now, the easiest way to do that was to find José Alvarez first.

Gillian asked in a small voice, "What are you going to do to me?"

"Don't be any dumber than you are," Carmody told her. "What would I do to you? I don't hurt little girls."

"I'm not a little girl—"

"Unless," he said, "they lie to me. But you haven't lied to me, right?"

"No," she said.

"I hope not. For your sake."

Carmody backed over to the door, took off the chain. He said sardonically, "Don't take any more acting jobs from strangers," and opened the door and went out.

Across the street from the apartment building was an open-air bar. Carmody paid a hundred pesetas for the use of their telephone. The savage midday heat sucked sweat out of him as he dialed a local number, spoke briefly to a man called Flores. He'd gotten Flores' name and number from Moncada, his Madrid contact, who had assured him Flores could be trusted and would be available if he needed any help.

Flores said it would take him twenty minutes to get to Calle Villalonga. Carmody rang off, sat at one of the interior tables that let him have an unobstructed view of the apartment complex. Two young women came out while he nursed a bottle of San Miguel; neither was Gillian Waltham.

At the end of twenty minutes, a small Seat pulled up outside and a slick-haired Spaniard in chinos and a striped T-shirt got out and came into the bar. He showed Carmody his teeth. "I am Flores, *señor*," he said as he sat down.

Carmody folded five thousand-peseta notes lengthwise. He said, "There's a girl in that building across the street," and described Gillian Waltham. "If she comes out, you follow her. If she heads for the airport, let her go but find out what flight she's leaving on. If she goes somewhere else, follow her until she stays put and then leave a message for me at American Express. Another thing: watch who goes into the building, and if you see a short, fat man with woolly gray hair, wait until he comes out and follow him. You got all that?"

"*Sí*, I have it, *señor*."

"Read it back to me."

Flores read it back, almost verbatim. Carmody slid the thousand-peseta notes across the table, got on his feet, and went out again into the vampiric heat.

TUESDAY,
LATE MORNING — SILVERA

The blond Norwegian girl rolled over in bed, drew the sheet away from her nude body, and watched Silvera with half-lidded eyes. "Diego," she said sleepily, "come and make love to me again."

He had just stepped out of the bathroom, a hotel towel tied around his waist. He looked at the girl, whose name was Brita, and said, "You were not satisfied last night and this morning?"

"Such a question!"

"And still you want more?"

"From you, Diego, oh yes."

Silvera laughed, went to where his carry-all rested on the luggage rack. He took out a fresh off-white gabardine suit, a dark blue shirt, a change of underwear and socks. Behind him, Brita said his name again, but he had forgotten her for the moment; he was thinking again of his telephone conversation with the *patrón* yesterday afternoon.

He had altered the details of Fanning's death to protect himself. But the *patrón* had gone into a rage anyway, shouting invectives like a child having a tantrum. He refused to listen to excuses, he wanted results, he wanted his diamonds! And so today he was flying to Majorca to take charge of matters personally.

That was fine with Silvera. He was no detective, he was not being paid to think, he had no idea how to go about finding Jennifer Evans. He did not know what she looked like; Fanning had carried no photographs in his wallet. There were thousands of hotels and *pensións* in Palma and the other island towns, as well as a great many private dwellings available on short notice; he could not canvass all of them, it was an impossible task. No, he would bring the diamonds, he would kill Jennifer Evans if it was required, but let the *patrón* decide how they were to be found.

After the call, he had driven Fanning's 600 Seat to a parking slot on the Borné and then taken a taxi out to the Calvia-Capdella Road. From there he had walked up the lane to Carmody's villa and retrieved his 1200 sedan. Back in Palma, in his room at the Melia Mallorca, he had bathed and changed clothes with a growing restlessness. He knew the restlessness for what it was—the need for a woman, desire awakened by the death of Fanning and the sight of Fanning's blood. So he had gone to El Terreno, made the rounds of the nightclubs and discotheques. He had found Brita almost immediately, in Tito's, and they had eaten *langusta* and drunk good Majorcan champagne, and before eleven they were in bed in his room.

Now, this morning, he felt sated—but until the diamonds were recovered, and the *patrón* was satisfied, he would not be able to fully relax and enjoy himself and Brita's fine young body. Still, there was no work to be done until the *patrón* arrived later in the day. Brita and her hungry flesh would serve to keep him occupied.

He closed the carry-all, then locked it because all of

Allen Fanning's personal effects were inside. The *patrón* wanted to see them, even though Silvera had assured him there was nothing to offer a lead to Jennifer Evans or the diamonds. Then he turned to look at Brita again.

She had been watching him, and now she stretched languidly without taking her eyes from his face, parting long legs, drawing one knee up. She began to stroke her sides, belly, thighs with the palm of one long-fingered hand. The other hand beckoned to him. "*Kjaere*," she murmured. "*Kjaere*, come to me."

Silvera moved to the bed, sat down beside her. Immediately she sat up and rubbed her breasts catlike against his chest. Her right hand unfastened the towel at his waist; her lips were warm and wet, nibbling at his ear.

He took her quickly the first time, lingeringly the second, and in his mind were pictures that would have filled the girl with revulsion if she had known what they were.

TUESDAY NOON – GILLIAN

After Carmody was gone, she sat on the couch and lighted a cigarette with unsteady hands. She felt strange, lightheaded. Fear was a dull thing now, moving sluggishly across the surface of her mind.

She shouldn't have lied to him. She should have told him the truth about Zaanhof, what had happened last night at Zaanhof's villa. But she had been afraid he would become angry, take out his frustration on her; he wanted Zaanhof *alive*. And she couldn't remember where the villa was. She hadn't paid any attention to the route they'd taken from the airport; and after she had killed . . . after Zaanhof died she had run blindly. She couldn't even remember leaving the villa or finding a taxi. All she remembered was getting out of a cab here at Liane's, with both of her bags in hand. Thank God some part of her had been aware enough to make her pick them up before her flight. Everything about last night was murky, unreal. Except the image of Zaanhof lying there dead, his staring eyes, the blood around his head; that was painfully sharp. It had robbed her of sleep most of the night.

What would happen when Carmody found out about Zaanhof? And he would, sooner or later; he was relentless. Would he come looking for her again? Would he know she'd been responsible and would he believe her if she told him the truth?

His eyes . . . those flat hard eyes! At first she'd thought they were cruel, that he was a cruel man. He was capable of violence, she was sure of that, but not in cold blood, not without a purpose. And not against a woman, unless he had greater provocation than she'd given him; he hadn't hurt her today, had he? He was full of menace but it was a kind of righteous menace—like a hanging judge. She'd seen a photograph once of Judge Roy Bean and that was how Carmody's eyes looked, just like the Old West magistrate's.

If only she could get out of Spain, go home where she'd be safe and she could forget about him and about Zaanhof. But she didn't have the two thousand dollars—she'd been too sick and terrified to remember the money until she was here at Liane's—and Liane didn't have the price of plane fare to the States, even if she'd known her well enough to borrow that much. Liane was just a girl who had come to Europe to play in the sun and who worked evenings as a hostess in one of Málaga's better restaurants. That was where they'd met, at the restaurant. Fernando had taken her there—

Fernando.

He wasn't poor, he might loan her enough money to . . . no. No. She couldn't go crawling to him, not after he'd used and discarded her the way he had. She couldn't stand to see him again. He wouldn't loan her a thousand dollars anyway, not that much. Why should he? Besides, he probably wasn't even in Málaga; he traveled a lot on business.

No, the only way she could get the money was to wire

her folks in Canton. They weren't well off; her dad might have to get a loan and that would take time and she hated the thought of asking them. But it was the only way. She could stay here with Liane until the money arrived. And hope Carmody didn't find Zaanhof and come back before it did.

Sweat oiled her face; under the collar of her blouse, the skin on her neck prickled with heat rash. She crushed out her cigarette, went into the tiny bathroom, ran cool water into the basin — not looking at herself in the mirror. She splashed water on her face and neck, took the rough towel off its wall hook.

It was while she was drying her bare wrists that she remembered the bracelet.

Sudden panic flared in her. Her bracelet, her silver bracelet! She dropped the towel and ran into the living room, into the bedroom, into the little kitchenette; it wasn't in any of them, it wasn't here.

"No!" she said aloud. "Oh God, no!"

She had been wearing the bracelet in Amsterdam, she had been wearing it on the plane with Zaanhof, she had been wearing it at his villa . . . *he had grabbed her arms, her wrists, held them tightly while his fat body thrust against hers* . . . she might have lost it afterward, it might have dropped off while she was running . . . *he had been holding onto her left arm when she first hit him with the statuette, she could feel again the pain of his fingers pulling at her as he staggered away, and the bracelet, the bracelet being torn loose* . . .

It was at his villa. No question, at his villa, lying on the floor somewhere near the dead thing that had once been Peter Zaanhof.

She could see the inscription on its back. Clearly in her mind, with a feeling of sick, warm horror.

To Gillian With All My Love — Grandmother Waltham.

TUESDAY AFTERNOON – CARMODY

The American Express office was just closing for the customary three-hour afternoon siesta when Carmody arrived. He talked his way inside, to find out if he had any messages. No messages, but there was a telegram. He claimed it with his passport, went out and read it in the shade of a palm tree.

It was from Van Hagen, and it said:

YOUR PARTY NAMED JORGE RIUYKEN. FORMER DIAMOND MERCHANT HERE BLACKLISTED 1959 FOR QUESTIONABLE DEALINGS. NOW UNLICENSED INDEPENDENT ENGAGED SAME BUSINESS PRIVATE COLLECTORS. SAID TO BE LIVING MALAGA BUT ADDRESS UNAVAILABLE YET. ONE KNOWN MALAGA ACQUAINTENCE THEO HUYMANS YACHT DIKKERT MALAGA YACHT CLUB. HUYMANS RETIRED BUSINESSMAN WELL

REGARDED HERE. BUSINESS DEALINGS WITH
RIUYKEN PRIOR 1959 BUT EVIDENTLY NONE SINCE.
SOLD HUGE PRIVATE DIAMOND COLLECTION
HERE BEFORE RETIRING TO SPAIN.

Carmody took another taxi, this one to the Avenida
del Generalissmo Franco; he picked up his rental Mercedes
and then drove to the harbor. The yacht *Dikkert* turned
out to be a 56-foot, broad-beamed, ocean-going vessel
fifteen or twenty years old; its brass fittings gleamed, its
hull was freshly painted, oil and varnish had been recently
applied to its decks and superstructure. On the rear deck,
ringed with planter boxes of bright red geraniums, an
elderly couple sat under an umbrella playing cards.

The man was Theo Huymans—slender, gray-maned,
friendly, English-speaking. Carmody told him his name
was Johnson, that he was trying to locate a friend of
Huymans'; he was invited aboard. Huymans shook his
hand, introduced him to his wife, offered a drink that
Carmody declined. He sensed no recognition in the man,
nothing hidden, no threat to himself. Huymans wasn't the
man behind Zaanhof/Riuyken; he was as sure of that as
he ever was of anything in his business.

Huymans said, "The name of the friend you are looking
for, Herr Johnson?"

"Jorge Riuyken."

"Ah, of course."

"It has to do with some gems—a business matter."

"Diamonds?"

"Yes."

"You are a collector?"

"No, an agent for one."

"Perhaps I know him too."

"Perhaps. But he prefers to remain anonymous."

Huymans smiled. "In matters of diamonds, that is often
wise. I was a collector myself once, you know."

"Yes, so I've been told."

"Now I am an old man who prefers cards, sunshine,

and cognac." He didn't sound bitter; he sounded happy.

"About Jorge Riuyken, Mr. Huymans."

"Yes. I haven't seen him in . . . oh, quite some time. Occasionally we have a meal together. We are both Dutch; there are not many Dutch in Málaga, you know—not many of our station, I should say."

"Does he live in the city?"

"On the outskirts, yes. My wife and I prefer our yacht to a villa. Jorge is hopelessly land-bound."

"Riuyken has a villa, then?"

"Oh yes. Quite a large villa."

"Would you mind telling me the address?"

Huymans gave that some thought. "Your business with him—it involves a large sum of money?"

"Several hundred thousand dollars."

"Ah." The old Dutchman smiled reminiscently. "Jorge once handled a transaction for me of that size. His commision was the largest he had earned up to that time. He was most grateful."

"He'll be grateful to you again for helping me," Carmody said. "His address, Heer Huymans?"

"Calle Sagrario," Huymans said. "Number thirty-two."

TUESDAY AFTERNOON — GILLIAN

It was a crazy idea. She knew it was a crazy idea but once it came to her she couldn't seem to get rid of it.

She had to get out of Málaga, didn't she? She couldn't just wire her folks and then sit here and wait for them to send her the money. There was no telling how soon Zaanhof's body would be found by the police. Or by one of his friends, maybe even the man who had ordered the ruse with the diamonds. If Carmody found it first . . . but she couldn't be sure he would. All she could be sure of was that if the police or Zaanhof's friends found that bracelet with her name on it, she faced a hideous future. They wouldn't believe her story of Zaanhof's attempted rape; too much time had passed, and she'd run away without reporting the death, and she had no proof that he had tried to attack her. Spanish justice was swift and merciless, for foreigners as well as natives. And she had heard Spanish prisons were hellholes, where all sorts of atrocities were committed.

A crazy idea, yes, and a big risk. But she didn't have any more to lose than if she stayed here and they caught her. And she didn't have anywhere else to go where she'd be safe even for a little while. It was just crazy enough to save her life and maybe get her out of Spain and eventually back home.

By the time Liane finally returned, late as usual, Gillian knew she was going to do it . . . if Liane was willing and able to help.

Liane said as she deposited two heavy bags of groceries on the kitchenette table, "I bought some cold meat and things. Are you hungry?"

"Not really, no."

"Are you still upset about last night?"

She'd told Liane that a man had tried to attack her near the *pensión* where she'd planned to spend the night, that it had shaken her so much she'd been afraid to stay anywhere alone. The lie was much better than the truth— and Liane had been sympathetic.

"A little, I suppose," she said.

"Well, you'll get over it. Things like that happen, even in Spain."

"Liane . . ."

"What, Gil?"

"Liane . . . can you let me have four thousand pesetas?"

The dark-haired girl looked at her steadily. "What for? I thought you had plenty of money to get home on."

"Well, I . . . I thought I did, but I don't. I checked air fares and with the connecting flights I'm going to need another sixty dollars . . ."

Liane took her gently by the shoulders. "There's something you're not telling me, isn't there? You're in some kind of trouble. What is it, Gil?"

"No," Gillian said too quickly. "Please, Liane, can you let me have the money? I'll pay you back as soon as I can, you know I will."

"You don't want to talk about it, then. Or you're afraid

to."

"It's nothing like that, there's nothing wrong."

"Yes, there is. If you tell me, maybe I can help—"

"You can help by loaning me four thousand pesetas."

"All right, Gil. I guess you know what you're doing. If you need the money that badly, it's yours."

She left the apartment at two o'clock, with her bags and the four thousand pesetas of Liane's money. A half-block away on Calle Villalonga, she found a taxi and told the driver to take her to the airport. He drove too fast through the hot afternoon, cutting in and out of the heavy traffic, and the recklessness of his pace gave Gillian an uneasy feeling of headlong flight from unseen pursuers. Nervously, she told him in English to slow down, but he didn't understand, or pretended not to. He swerved in front of a truck, ran a caution light at an intersection, narrowly missed a tour bus that had crept out from the right-hand curb. Gillian closed her eyes, braced herself on the sweating leather seat.

She had never felt more alone in her life.

TUESDAY AFTERNOON – CARMODY

Carmody parked the rented Mercedes on the winding street above Calle Sagrario, made sure he was unobserved before crossing to pine and cypress trees on the far side. He went down through the trees until he could see the white-stone villa nestled below. It was number 32; he'd made a pass in front to identify it before coming up here.

The descent to the rear of the villa was steep; he took his time to keep from losing his footing and to keep from making noise. The back terrace, overgrown with mastic and orange trees, stretched to the base of another steep slope and was enclosed by a rambling, waist-high brick wall. The pines and cypress extended close to the wall on the side where he was.

When he was ten feet from the wall Carmody stopped behind the bole of a pine to look and listen. The windows along that side of the villa were shuttered, but he could see an unprotected set of louvered wooden doors under a rear archway. There was nothing to hear except the hot wind.

He moved ahead to the terrace wall, climbed over it. The Beretta was in his hand now, held down low along his right leg. He worked his way across the terrace to the archway where the wooden doors were. When he raised up to look through the down-slanted louvers he could see most of the way to the front entrance. The passage was deserted. But there were lights on somewhere inside; he could see the faint glow of them at the upper edge of the hallway. At this time of day, lights on and shutters fastened down made little sense.

Carmody didn't like it. Something was wrong here; he could feel it already. He looked at the joining of the two doors, saw no keyhole, and judged that they were locked by a simple bar arrangement. There wasn't much crime in Spain, with the Franco dictatorship's stiff penalties for breaking the law, so people didn't secure their houses the way they did in other countries. He stepped back, then drove his right foot against the joining midway up.

The two halves burst apart, inward. Carmody ran through the opening with the gun up in his hand, along the hallway to where a massive living room opened up. The living room was where the light was coming from. He put his back against the wall there, eased his head around for a look.

He saw the dead man immediately, sprawled on his back between a couch and the fireplace. Eyes open and staring, dried blood staining the tiles around his head. The tubby little Dutchman, Jorge Riuyken.

Carmody said, "Shit!" bitterly and savagely. For a few seconds he stayed where he was, listening; the house had the thick hot hush of desertion. He went into the living room, knelt beside the man who had called himself Peter Zaanhof. Dead a long time—rigor come and gone. Even in this heat, that meant last night sometime, early last night.

He turned the corpse slightly, saw the fingernail

scratches on the neck, the bruise marks where Riuyken had been hit with something heavy. He peered at the wound at the base of the skull, then straightened and looked the room over. Matted blood and hair on a corner of the low table nearby. Signs of a struggle. Olive-wood statuette on the floor in front of the fireplace; blood on that too. And something else over there, something silver gleaming in the light. He picked it up, recognized it even before he read the inscription etched into its back side: the dangly bracelet Gillian Waltham had worn the whole time in Amsterdam.

So she'd lied to him after all. Came here last night with Riuyken, after they got in from The Netherlands, and that damn fat Dutchman had made a pass and she wasn't having any. Clawed him when he pressed it and then hit him with the statuette. He'd gone down, cracked the back of his head hard enough on that low table to kill himself. And she'd panicked and run to the girl friend. From the lay of the room, the physical evidence, that was how it shaped up.

But *was* that all there was to it? Why hadn't she told him what had happened? Fear, maybe; and maybe some other reason. If she'd lied about that much, it could be she'd lied about some of the rest of it too—like about knowing who was behind Zaanhof/Riuyken and what the game was all about.

Carmody put the bracelet into his jacket pocket, paused without thinking about it to wipe off the bloody statuette, then searched the house. It was as empty as he'd felt it to be. He found a telephone in Riuyken's study, sat on the edge of a desk with an oxblood-colored veneer, and dialed the number of the bar across from Liane Butler's apartment house.

Flores was gone. The barman remembered him, said that he'd left hurriedly half an hour ago. Carmody slammed the receiver down, immediately picked it up again and dialed American Express. There was no answer; they were still shut down for siesta. He banged the handset down for the second time, swung around the desk, sat in the black leather chair behind it, and began going through the drawers.

The right-hand bottom drawer was locked; none of the others told him anything. He tried to jimmy the locked one, but it resisted his attempts. He returned to the living room, went through Riuyken's pockets, found a ring of keys. He also turned up a fat wallet. He pocketed the keys and opened the wallet.

It contained identification cards, all in the name of Jorge Riuyken; a snapshot of Riuyken and a dark-skinned redhead who looked like a whore; a pornographic color photo of a man and two teen-age girls; several thousand pesetas in large notes; and two thousand American dollars in fifties and hundreds.

Two thousand dollars. The price Gillian had claimed was her fee. This was the payoff money, probably—the bait to get her here last night. She must have panicked after Riuyken died; otherwise she'd have gone through his pockets, and seen the bracelet on the floor as well. Another point in her favor.

He took the fifties and hundreds out of the Dutchman's wallet and tucked them away inside his own. Maybe he'd give the money and the bracelet to her later on, depending on what she had to say and how he felt about her at the time. Why he should bother—why he'd bothered to wipe her prints off the statuette—he didn't know and didn't want to think about.

He replaced Riuyken's billfold and then went through the rest of the dead man's clothing without finding anything that interested him. Back in the study, he found that the smallest key on the ring opened the locked desk drawer. Inside the drawer was an accordion file containing miscellaneous correspondence, bills, receipts, bank statements—all of it useless to his purpose.

Carmody studied the other keys on the ring. Two were unusual: long, heavy, with nearly but not quite identical sets of grooves. Safe deposit keys? No, they were too heavy for that. But maybe . . .

He stood and began to prowl the room. It took him ten minutes to find the safe: it was set into the floor and concealed under a long planter box full of ferns, beneath one of the windows. A little dirt on the floor, from the last time the planter was moved, led him to it.

With the box out of the way, Carmody knelt and examined the safe door. Circular, about eighteen inches in diameter, set flush with the floor. Made of heavy steel. Pull ring in the center, two recessed key slots on either side.

The two long flat keys fitted into the slots, but when he tried turning first one and then the other, the safe remained locked. It worked in some kind of sequence, then. He spent another five minutes of trial and error working it out: left key one half turn clockwise; right key one full turn counterclockwise. When he tugged on the ring, the door lifted and stayed raised on its hinges.

Money—two thick packets of both pesetas and U.S. dollars. And a large alphabetized file made of twin metal loops set into a flat base; more than fifty 4 x 5 cards were strung over the loops.

Carmody carried the file over to the desk where the light was better. Each card contained the names and addresses of men—and a couple of women—in several European countries, England, Canada, the U.S., Brazil. Diamond merchants, collectors, contacts, probably. If Riuyken had been dealing with all these people, he'd had a nice little cottage industry going.

All right. But was one of these names the man who had ordered the Amsterdam ruse? If Gillian Waltham's story could be believed, the plan had been hurriedly concocted and carried out; she had been approached, briefed, and sent on her way to Majorca within thirty-six hours. With the phony diamonds. Quality synthetics were something a man like Riuyken might keep on hand; but if he'd supplied them, why hadn't he given them to the girl immediately, had her sew them into her bra herself? Didn't trust her, maybe. Or maybe they *hadn't* come from

Riuyken but from the boss man.

If that was the case, then the boss man had to live somewhere nearby—somewhere in Spain, or Portugal or North Africa, at the outside. There hadn't been enough time for a lengthy trip to pick up the synthetics or to have them delivered. That was a big *if*, a longshot, but he didn't have any better parlay. In the absence of a sure thing, play a longshot; sometimes you got lucky and it came in.

He found a pen and a piece of paper, then went through the file cards again. When he'd flipped over the last one he had a list of eight names and addresses in Spain and one in Lisbon. Five of the eight were in Barcelona, Madrid, and Pamplona; the other three were in closer proximity to Málaga.

Carlos Miralles, Torremolinos.

Albert Opdehyde, Algeciras.

Jaime Rosellon, Mirabela.

There was no way to know whether the three were buyers, sellers, or contacts; Riuyken hadn't marked the cards in any way. But the addresses, wealthy areas along the Costa del Sol, tipped the scales in favor of private collectors, men with money. Might as well start with those three first.

He put the file away, closed and locked the safe, replaced the planter box, returned the keys to the dead Dutchman's pocket, and went to play his first longshot.

TUESDAY AFTERNOON – CARMODY

Torremolinos was queen of the Spanish Sun Coast, the place where the jet-setters and the film stars and starlets and the idle rich went to play. Scenic cliffs, luxury hotels, sprawling villas, million-dollar yachts anchored in the harbor, beaches overflowing with lush women and bronzed men from a dozen different countries. Even though it was only eight kilometers from Málaga, Torremolinos was worlds apart. You could see, feel, smell, touch, taste the money there. And the two fluids that flowed most frequently, one cold, one hot, were champagne and semen.

If Málaga was the asshole of Spain, neighboring Torremolinos was the country's lusty genitalia.

Carmody didn't like it any better. It was just as hot and just as crowded and just as noisy and even more overpriced. He didn't understand the kind of life that went on there, he didn't fit into it, and it made him uncomfortable when he had to deal with it. Business didn't bring him to Torremolinos often, just as it didn't often bring him to Málaga. He'd have been happy if it never brought him to either town again.

On the outskirts of the village he stopped at a small *pensión*. The *pensiónes* tended to be run by friendlier— and hungrier—people than the larger hotels. The woman behind the desk of this one was more than willing to let Carmody use her telephone, and to offer him whatever information he wanted, when he laid the five-hundred-peseta note in front of her. Did she know where the Villa Miralles was located? Oh, *sí, señor*, everyone knew the Villa Miralles and the Señor Carlos Miralles; he lived on one of the jagged cliffs two kilometers back toward Málaga. The road to his villa was private and one kilometer in length. No, *señor*, there was no gate barring entrance.

Carmody put in a call to the American Express office in Málaga. It was open now, and there was a message for him from the young Spaniard, Flores; he was to call the number Moncada had given him originally. Carmody had the operator get him the number. Flores came on the line on the second ring.

Carmody said, "Where did the girl go?"

"To the airport, *señor*. She took a taxi driven by a crazy man and I was unable to stay with them in the traffic. But she had two suitcases and I surmised—"

"Never mind all that. Was she at the airport when you got there?"

"No, *señor*. Her plane had already departed."

"So you found out where she went?"

"*Sí*. To Palma de Mallorca."

"Palma? Are you sure?"

"Yes, *señor*. Positive."

Carmody put down the receiver. Why would Gillian go to Majorca? He was sorry, now, he hadn't told Flores to follow her wherever she went. Her flying to Palma made no sense to him.

He left the *pensión*, drove back along the two-lane highway, found the private road to the Villa Miralles.

Climbing, he passed between thick growths of bamboo and scrub palm, over and through which he had glimpses of the Mediterranean. The road, surfaced with crushed white rock, rose sharply, hooking left, and finally he could see the estate ahead.

The term "villa" was a misnomer in this case. Moorish in design, it was the kind of patrician country house known in Spain as a *palacio rural*. Carmody had seen the type before, in the extreme coastal and fashionable interior sections of Majorca. The face of the cliff on which it sat was flat and oval-shaped; house and grounds took up three-quarters of the space. The other quarter was a parking area made of the same crushed white rock as the road—empty now except for a small gray Citröen parked nose up to one of the concrete abutments that marked the cliff's edge. A low, pastel-colored wall, with a black iron gate set in its middle, separated the parking area from the estate grounds; beyond it Carmody could see yew trees and a junglelike garden dotted with ironwork sculptures.

As he pulled onto the parking area, a short, wiry man wearing a sports shirt and knife-crease slacks came walking through the gate. The man took several steps toward the Citröen, then stopped when he heard the sound of the Mercedes' engine. His head turned out of profile; sunlight limned his sharp-featured face.

José Alvarez.

Carmody's lips pulled in against his teeth in a wolfish grimace. He slid his foot off the brake and onto the accelerator, spinning the wheel; the Mercedes responded into a long, slewing arc that cut Alvarez off from the Citröen. Startled, Alvarez stood frozen a few seconds longer—until he could see into the Mercedes well enough to recognize Carmody. His expression of surprise turned into one of terror. He threw a wild look over his shoulder, saw that the gate was too far away, and broke into a spindle-legged run toward the edge of the cliff. When he got there he sidestepped one of the abutments, disappeared beyond the rim.

Carmody had the door open before he brought the Mercedes to a full stop. He jerked on the emergency brake and came out running. When he reached the edge he saw that a steep, sandy path wound down the cliff wall to a narrow private beach. Alvarez was scrambling down the path, using his hands on juts of cliff rock to keep his balance.

Carmody's eyes glittered. The longshot had come in, the first one he'd played for a lucky change—and the payoff was going to be better than he'd expected, too.

He glanced at the *palacio* but no one else was in sight. With the Beretta drawn, he went down the path at a skidding run. Immediately he began to gain on the Spaniard: Alvarez's fear was making him clumsy and swivel-necked. He was three-quarters of the way down when Alvarez reached the bottom and jumped the last five feet and fell sprawling onto the rocky sand. Alvarez got his legs under him, ran toward the far cliff wall. But there was nowhere for him to go. The beach was bounded on three sides by the bluff wall and on the other by the Mediterranean. He came to the end of the beach as Carmody reached the path's end; stopped, turned, rolled his eyes in all directions, and then took three steps toward the sea as if he were thinking of trying to swim for it.

Carmody shouted, "Stay out of the water, Alvarez, or I'll blow your fucking head off!"

Alvarez made an unintelligible sound that carried across the stillness. In little crablike steps he backed away from the water, diagonally toward the cliff wall, as Carmody approached him in long, hard strides. When his spine touched the wall he stopped and stood with his hands braced against the rock on either side, his face gray and wet and miserable.

Without slowing Carmody went up to him and slapped him across the face, forehand and backhand, twice. Alvarez fell to his knees, knelt in the pebbled sand with his arms extended, palms outward. "*Señor, por favor, no me matar, Madre de Dios no me matar!*" His voice was a shrill, liquid whine.

Carmody wrapped fingers in the front of the man's shirt, hauled him to his feet, shoved him back against the cliff. He pressed the Beretta's muzzle against the quivering jaw, held it there. "Talk to me, Alvarez," he said, "and maybe I won't kill you. Tell me things."

"*Sí, sí, sí, sí!*"

"We'll start with Miralles. Who is he?"

"*Un hombre de negocios jubilado,*" Alvarez said. Sweat rolled thickly along his cheeks. "*Muy poderoso . . .*"

"In English, José, so I'll be sure to understand."

"A retired businessman, a powerful and important man —a bad man."

"Yes? Why would this bad man want to play games with me?"

"The diamonds . . ."

"What diamonds? Not the synthetics Riuyken gave the girl."

"No, no, real diamonds, fine diamonds worth more than twenty million pesetas."

Carmody stared at him. That was better than three hundred thousand dollars, American. He said, "Hot ice?"

Alvarez started to shake his head, thought better of the movement with the gun tight against his jaw. "These . . . these diamonds are the property of Miralles, he is a collector of diamonds, it is said he is obsessed with them, values them above all else . . ."

Carmody said, "How do these stones tie up with me?"

"They were stolen by a man named Fanning, employed by Miralles as a secretary."

"Yes? Keep talking."

Alvarez said, "Five days ago, Fanning telephoned me. He said he wished to be put in contact with you, that he wished to arrange for your professional services. I believed at first he was calling for Miralles."

"How did Fanning know you?"

"I have supplied Miralles with women—he gives many parties and his guests sometimes desire company. I would make the arrangements with Fanning."

"All right. And how did he know about me?"

"Your reputation. Fanning was close to Miralles, and to the friends of Miralles . . . a chance remark, an overheard conversation . . . you see?"

"I'm beginning to," Carmody said.

"When I asked Fanning to explain why he wished your services, he said it was to see to the safe transportation of two persons and something of great value to a distant place. I told him that you would want to know the details, but he was evasive. He would tell you and only you, he said. There was one other condition—that his meeting with you would be at a place of his choosing. I was not to contact him for any reason; he would call again to learn if the terms were acceptable to you."

"But you never did call me, did you. Why?"

"I was suspicious of Fanning's motives," Alvarez said. "And your instructions to me, Señor Carmody . . . always to be most careful with potential clients, *no es verdad?*"

"So you decided to talk to Miralles personally."

"*Sí.* Yes. He was very upset. He demanded to know where Fanning was but of course I couldn't tell him."

"Disappeared with the diamonds," Carmody said.

"Yes. Miralles said I must help him find Fanning, and when I refused he threatened me, he—"

"—offered you money."

Alvarez said plaintively, "I had no choice but to do his bidding. Miralles is a bad man, a very bad and powerful man."

"You already said that, José."

"Señor Carmody, I swear this, I did not think then that you would ever be involved."

"Get on with your story."

Alvarez drew a ragged breath, let it out with a sound like a snake hissing. "Miralles instructed me to tell Fanning you had agreed to meet with him—but that you would name the place of this meeting. Fanning would not agree. He was afraid of a trap. He said the only meeting place acceptable to him was your villa."

"He knew where I lived?"

"Somehow he had found out. He also knew he could not approach you directly, without first going through me or another of your contacts. That you would not see him if he tried. When I spoke again with Miralles he said we must do as Fanning wished—it was the only way to bring Fanning and the diamonds into the open quickly. So we must arrange for you to be drawn away from Majorca so your villa could be used."

Carmody said thinly, "By sending somebody to break in and then to impersonate me, is that it?"

"Yes."

"Who? Not Miralles himself?"

"No. An agent . . . I do not know who. Señor Carmody, I begged Miralles to reconsider. But he would not. He knew you could not be paid to betray Fanning, to allow your home to be used in such a fashion. And he . . . he did not dare to risk any other means of dealing with you."

"Killing me or kidnapping me, you mean."

"I would not allow that, señor. You must believe me. If Miralles had insisted upon such measures I would have defied him, I would have contacted you immediately—"

"Sure you would have, José."

"He assured me you would not be harmed. A simple ruse to take you to Amsterdam for two days, you would be well paid, and when you returned all at your villa would be as you had left it. You would never know the truth."

"Except that Jorge Riuyken couldn't or wouldn't raise enough money to make the Amsterdam payoff look good and made the big mistake of pulling a gun on me and locking me in a closet. That mistake is going to cost everybody concerned, one way or another."

"A fool, Riuyken, an arrogant fool—"

"A dead fool, now," Carmody said.

Alvarez rolled his eyes upward, saw that Carmody meant it, and began to shake. He muttered something in Spanish that might have been a prayer.

"How was Fanning set up?" Carmody asked him. "Give me the details."

"Señor Carmody, please, please . . ."

Carmody shut that off with pressure from the Beretta. "The details, José."

They came out of Alvarez in fits and starts. Riuyken had contacted Gillian—Alvarez didn't know how he'd gotten her name—and once she agreed, he'd called Miralles and Miralles had called Alvarez. Alvarez set up the Saturday meet between Carmody and Gillian—and when Fanning got in touch with him again, he'd stalled him until Saturday afternoon to make sure the girl was successful in getting Carmody to Amsterdam. Then, on Fanning's next call, Alvarez had tried to arrange the trap at Carmody's villa for Sunday; but Fanning wanted it on Monday morning instead, so they'd had to keep Carmody and Gillian hanging an extra day in Amsterdam.

Carmody said, "What happened yesterday at my villa?"

"I do not know, I did not ask."

"Did they kill Fanning at my villa?"

"Señor, I swear I don't know—"

"No, you little shit, you wouldn't want to know, would you? But Miralles knows, by God. Where is he? Up there in his *palacio*?"

"No. No, he went away."

"Went where?"

"To Majorca."

"Why?"

"I do not know," Alvarez said. "I spoke with one of his servants—there is no one at the *palacio* but servants. He said Miralles was upset. He didn't know why."

"Something to do with Fanning and the diamonds?"

"Perhaps, but I don't—"

"Don't know, yeah. Does he have a house on the island?"

"I have never heard one mentioned."

"Where does he usually stay? Which hotel?"

"I have no idea, I swear—"

"When did he leave here?"

"This afternoon, two hours ago."

"Why did *you* come out here, José? Why did you leave Barcelona?"

"Señor Carmody, you must believe me, I did not want to become involved in this treachery, I did not wish to betray you, but I had no choice. Miralles gave me no choice. He is a bad man, a bad man, he would have killed me as he would a fly. I came for the money I was promised, I am going to Portugal, I knew you would blame me and come looking for me and I was afraid . . ."

Alvarez kept on babbling, pleading, but Carmody had quit listening. He was thinking about Miralles, about the set-up. If the agent he'd sent to the villa had met Fanning and gotten the diamonds, then disposed of Fanning, why had Miralles gone to Majorca today? To pick up his diamonds? Maybe—but why wouldn't he have just had them delivered by the agent? And why had he been upset when he'd left? A man obsessed with diamonds wouldn't be upset if he'd just recovered twenty million pesetas' worth stolen from his collection. Maybe something had gone wrong, then; maybe the diamonds hadn't been recovered, or Fanning was still on the loose, or both.

Alvarez said piteously, "Please, Señor Carmody, you will not kill me? I was forced to betray you, I was *forced*. Please, I beg of you—"

"Begging is the way you'll eat from now on," Carmody told him flatly, "if I have anything to say about it. You're through in my business, in Spain and Portugal both; I'll see to that. In six months you'll be pimping for five-dollar whores in the Lisbon slums."

He took the Beretta away from Alvarez's jaw, caught him by the ear, and wrenched him to his knees. Alvarez screamed, clapped both hands to the side of his head, cradling his injured ear. Carmody went away along the beach without looking back.

TUESDAY,
LATE AFTERNOON – MIRALLES

Carlos Miralles was a rich and powerful man because in his youth, during Spain's bloody Civil War, he had been a Socialist, a terrorist, a murderer, and a thief.

When King Alfonso was formally outlawed near the end of 1931, and Spain became a republic, Miralles had been twenty years old and, like many of his generation, a left-wing political zealot. He took part in the burning of churches and convents in his native Málaga, and with equal fervor denounced the Monarchists and President Zamora of the new central-right regime; later, after the 1933 general elections which swept the Popular Front into power, he became a member of the militant, extreme-left paramilitary formation that was being openly trained at the time. And at the outbreak of war in July of 1936, while Franco directed the uprising in Spanish Morocco and other insurgents fostered attacks in Madrid, Seville, Burgos, and Saragossa, Miralles was instrumental in the insurrection that made a bloodbath of Málaga.

By then he had risen to the rank of lieutenant and he led much of the street fighting against the Falangists and the Loyalists. He ordered the massacre of prisoners, guided bands of armed terrorists that entered private homes and slaughtered Loyalist sympathizers. It was a source of pride to him that he had personally shot and then decapitated six men in the name of Franco's newly organized Rebel government, the Junta de Nacional.

Málaga fell to the Rebels in February of 1937. Although large numbers of his fellow officers—Miralles was then a captain—left shortly after the victory to join Franco's siege on Madrid, he remained in the city by choice and manipulation. He had absolute authority there, his first taste of power. But the main reason he stayed was greed.

Miralles had been born into poverty, had joined the Socialists for this reason, had fought in the beginning for this reason. The hunger in his belly had long since been appeased, but the hunger in his soul for wealth and greater stature burned hot. There in Málaga, in mid-1937, he saw his opportunity to prepare for a luxurious post-war future. And he seized it.

Most of Spain's wealthy were supporters of the Rebels, or Nationalists as they were later called; but many influential families in and around Málaga had been or secretly still were Loyalists, and the spoils of war were available for the taking. Miralles embarked on a campaign of terrorism to ferret out suspected Loyalists—condemning them to death while he privately looted their valuables. Even this was not enough to satisfy him. On one occasion he murdered a German military adviser who had confided that he owned a priceless gold urn. On another occasion he denounced a confirmed Nationalist as a Republican, had him shot, and then stole two valuable paintings from the man's home. He had no religion, he had no conscience; the prosperity of Carlos Miralles was all that mattered to him.

In December of 1938, Franco launched a heavy offensive against the republic and within a month Barcelona had fallen and the Republican armies began to disintegrate. Three months later, when Franco marched victoriously into Madrid, the Civil War was over. More than a million Spaniards had died, Spain lay ravaged and desolate—and Carlos Miralles had assembled a fortune stained with the blood of his countrymen.

As an acclaimed hero of the insurrection, he was offered a political post in Franco's reconstruction program. He accepted, and over the next seven years, from beginning to end of World War II, he dedicated himself to the rebuilding of Málaga and its neighboring towns—and to furthering his own cause. He used his political position in Jekyll and Hyde fashion: instituting programs for the good of the people, supervising reconstruction projects; intimidating, threatening, and in one case killing to fatten his private horde. But he was only biding his time. This war would end too, eventually, and for his purpose it did not matter whether the Axis or the Allies emerged the victor. He had evolved a plan that would transform him from a well-to-do provincial politician into the wealthy giant of his dreams.

Early in 1945, with the defeat of the Axis a certainty, he began making private preparations for the establishment of his own import-export firm. With his political connections, he had no difficulty arranging to buy up the export rights to various types of leather goods. When peace came to Europe the following year, he resigned his government post and entered the business world.

His intention had not been to realize large capital gains from leather exports, but to use his company as a front for the secret distribution of artwork and other war spoils to America, South America, and the rebuilding countries of Europe. His storehouse was exhausted in two years—but by then he had also acquired a Midas touch in the business world. In the booming postwar market, his company's profits quickly doubled, tripled, quadrupled, until by 1951 it became one of the largest exporters in

Spain.

Miralles ran the firm with an iron hand, seeking ever-larger profits, until a developing heart condition forced him to retire in 1962. By then he had forgotten forever poverty and Socialism; had built his massive *palacio* outside Torremolinos and filled it with legitimately purchased works of art, beautiful mistresses, a large staff of servants.

And diamonds. Above all else, diamonds.

He had first discovered the gem during the Civil War, when he was looting the Loyalist rich of Málaga. Immediately, they became for him a symbol of wealth and power. He found that he could stare at a diamond, fascinated, for hours at a time; and that the feel of one was more exciting than the skin of a naked woman. Diamonds were never cold to Carlos Miralles; they were hot, hot, and the pain of their heat was the sweet pain of orgasm.

He acquired more diamonds as the years passed— individual stones, rings, necklaces, brooches, bracelets, earrings. They were the only commodity he did not sell on the black market after the end of World War II. And as he grew more and more wealthy, he bought more and more diamonds, spending millions of pesetas annually, employing dozens of men world-wide. In the *palacio* he had constructed two large burglar-proof diamond rooms for the display of his collection, and lighted them so brightly that the dazzle of so many carats was like a fire against the eyes.

The diamond rooms were sealed vaults to which he alone had the combinations; he had no fear of theft. But he had not taken into account the human factor. He had hired Allen Fanning as his social secretary because it was fashionable to have social secretaries and the man's references were impeccable. He grew to trust the mild-mannered, servile Britisher as much as he ever trusted anyone, and it had made him careless enough to allow Fanning to handle some minor diamond purchases. And suddenly, for no reason that Miralles could fathom,

Fanning had betrayed his trust and stolen twenty million pesetas' worth of cut and polished stones.

Now Fanning, the betrayer, the kidnapper, was dead.

But the diamonds, the children, part of the life's blood of Carlos Miralles, were still missing.

It was intolerable. Men had died, at his hands and his direction, for less offense than this.

More men than Fanning would die now if his diamonds were not found and safely returned.

He sat stiffly in his presidential suite at the Hotel Mallorca Grande, still lean and powerfully built at the age of sixty-two, and glared at Diego Silvera with eyes as bright as the gems he coveted. "Tell me again, Diego," he said, "what you have done to find this woman, this Jennifer Evans."

Silvera shifted in his chair. "I called at the minimum of one hundred hotels, *patrón*. I spoke with realtors, with the empolyees of car rental agencies. No one knows of her. And I could not describe her because I have no idea what she looks like. Fanning carried no photographs. It is possible Jennifer Evans is not her real name, or if it is, that she is using another. It is also possible that she has already left the island, much as I do not like to say it."

"I would be very upset if she has left Majorca with my diamonds, Diego."

"*Patrón*, I have done everything possible—"

"You should not have killed Fanning prematurely. You should have waited until you had the diamonds."

"It was unavoidable," Silvera said. "He fought like a wild man, he—"

"I want my diamonds. I do not want excuses."

Silvera spread his hands. "Tell me how to find them and I will do so. One man can only—"

"Tell you how to find them!" Miralles was abruptly on his feet, his face darkening. "I *told* you how to find them, five days ago; all the arrangements were made and your assignment a simple one, so simple a child could have accomplished it. Son of a whore, I do not have my diamonds because of you and now you wish me to do the task for which you were hired and which you failed!"

Defensive anger flashed in Silvera's eyes, but it was as brief as the flare of a match; he lowered his gaze. "I am sorry, *patrón*. Truly sorry."

Miralles stood staring down at him, his hands clenched. He started to speak again, but in his chest there was a tightness, a vague ache—and he remembered his heart, the warning of his doctor to avoid undue stress. With effort he calmed himself, returned to his chair. He sat drawing deep, slow breaths until the constriction in his chest eased, the pain vanished.

He said then, "Did you bring Fanning's possessions with you as I asked?"

"Yes, *patrón*."

Silvera had them in his coat pocket; he brought them to Miralles, laid them on the smoking table beside his chair. Miralles examined them carefully. He read each card in the wallet—his command of English was as fluent as Silvera's—and peered at keys, comb, handkerchief. Then, frowning, he said in English, "The secretary."

"¿Cómo?"

"Fanning's notebook, a small leatherbound notebook," Miralles said. "He called it his secretary—the secretary of a secretary, he would say. I never knew him to be without it; it contains telephone numbers, addresses, instructions, a memorandum calendar."

"I found no such notebook on his person."

"It might have fallen from his pocket."

"I searched the area before I buried him," Silvera said. "There was no notebook."

"With Fanning there was *always* the notebook. He went nowhere without it—nowhere, Diego."

"But I searched carefully, *patrón*. I would have found such a book if there had been one."

"Would you? There is no possibility you might have overlooked it?"

"None."

"I think differently," Miralles said. "I think you are a fool and a *pendejo*. I would not hire you again to shovel dog dung from my patio."

Silvera's lips thinned but he said nothing.

"Unfortunately you are the only person available to me at this moment. I will give you one last chance to redeem yourself. You will return to Carmody's villa and you will find Allen Fanning's secretary. Do not dare to come back here until you do."

"But what if Carmody has returned? He must surely have returned by this time—"

"If he is there, do what is necessary. Kill him if that is the only way. I no longer care about Carmody, Carmody is your problem. I care only about my diamonds."

"Killing Carmody would not be wise, *patrón*."

"Who are you to tell me what is wise? Kill him or do not kill him, but I will expect you to find Fanning's secretary, find Jennifer Evans, and find my diamonds."

"Even if I should find the secretary, there may be nothing in it to tell the whereabouts of Jennifer Evans."

"You must hope that there is, Diego. You must pray to your God there is."

"Are you threatening me, *patrón*?" Silvera asked softly.

"Yes, I am threatening you. Does this displease you, Diego? Do you wish to make an issue of it?"

Miralles locked gazes with the younger man—and it was Silvera, as was always the case in a clash of wills with underlings, who looked away first. But there was still defiance in Silvera. Even though he stood and went to the door, he stopped with his hand on the knob and turned and looked at Miralles again. "I will do what you ask, *patrón*," he said, "but if there is nothing to be found, I will not be held responsible. I am not afraid of you." He opened the door and went out, shutting it gently behind him.

"Son of a whore," Miralles said to the closed door. "Raper of mothers and nuns. If you fail me this time I will have you castrated, I will spit on your *cojones* and feed them to the gulls."

He took the huge diamond ring from his left index finger, held it close to his face, and caressed it. It burned him sweetly with its fire, and soothed him, and took away some of the ache that had come back into his chest . . .

TUESDAY,
EARLY EVENING – JENNIFER

In the hot, silent desolation of the farmhouse, Jennifer felt like screaming.

It was her nerves and it was the waiting and it was the bloody deafening hush in which nothing moved and nothing happened. Sitting on an ancient string-bottom chair, she had watched the sun set the night before, and the darkness come; and after a short and fitful sleep fogged with nightmare, she had watched the sun rise, and the heat crawl in liquid waves over the landscape, and the sun drift again across the sky. Waiting for nothing; hoping with a feeling of hopelessness; afraid to stay here but not quite able to make herself leave.

She clasped her hands over her breasts, bit down hard on her lower lip in an effort to still the inner jangling of her nerves. The silent scream lay heavy in the back of her throat. And yet, she felt none of the panic of the day before; her thoughts today were dull, sluggish, wrapped in a thick fabric of frustration and self-pity.

Early that morning she had told herself: I shouldn't have done it, I shouldn't have got involved in a crime, I should have said no to Allen and gone straight back to England. Poor old Allen, poor lovesick Allen, I'm as big a failure as he. And there's no sense in pretending any longer, I don't care a whit for him, I ask myself over and over where is, what has happened to him, but I simply don't care that much if he's alive or dead. It was the security, it was what he could buy for me. But you know, Jennie, if you'd gone home you might have found someone well off in spite of past disappointments, you truly might have; if you can get to London you might still find someone like that. But how can I go back now, with no money, trapped here and alone? Well, you can, you know, you can just walk out of here, hitchhike into Palma where there are jobs to be had, men to be had, you *can* get enough money to go home, Jennie. Then that's just what I'll do, I'll pack my clothes up and walk out of here right now because there's no point in staying, I can't find the diamonds—

—damn the filthy diamonds—

—but they might be here after all, I might have missed them somehow, if I can find them they'll be mine, all mine . . .

And so she'd stayed, alternately watching the day pass and re-searching the house, wanting to leave, not finding the diamonds, not leaving. And now another night was coming . . .

Abruptly she stood and entered the bedroom for the fiftieth time, aimlessly, to stand among the strewn articles of clothing and furnishings she had examined and re-examined. The sheets on the old-fashioned, iron-framed bed were pulled away, and the jagged incisions she had made in the mattress with a kitchen knife leaked stuffing like puffs of white blood. She stared at the bed—and found herself remembering the last night she'd spent there with Allen.

They had made love, and afterward he had said, "It won't be long now, love. Our own bed in our own house, with everything you've ever dreamed of at your fingertips." And she had said, "Silks and satins, laces and furs." And he had said, "Anything, dearest, anything at all . . ."

The memory made anger swell inside, then explosive fury. She picked up one of her blouses, one of Allen's shirts, a pair of panties, tore them viciously into tatters, flung the remains onto the floor; she ripped an ancient picture off the wall and battered it against the chest of drawers and pushed the chest over on its side and then began clawing stuffing out of the ruined mattress, panting, sobbing. Then, as quickly as it had come, the sudden violence left her and in its place was a despair so dark that she began to cry brokenly. Her legs felt weak, and weeping she sank onto the mattress and laid her head against the iron bed frame, one hand clinging to the ornamental knob that jutted up phallically from the corner.

The knob turned slightly in her grasp.

At first she didn't notice it; then, as the sharp edge of her suffering dulled, she realized that the knob was loose. Her head came up slowly. She dried her eyes with a clump of mattress stuffing, and turned the knob and found that it was screwed into its base, and unscrewed it all the way until it came off in her hand. Quickly she scooted over and looked into the cavity.

The leather pouch containing the diamonds was wedged inside.

Jennifer stared at the pouch for several seconds, then made a keening sound in her throat and dug feverishly into the cavity, breaking one of her nails, pulling the bag free, fumbling it open, spilling the glittering stones into her palm. She began to laugh, a sobbing, hiccuping sound. Closed her eyes and pressed the diamonds against her breasts, rocking back and forth.

Oh Allen, she thought, why didn't you tell me, right here in the bed, right here all the time while we made love. You should have told me, pet, but I forgive you, I do forgive you. You stole them for me and now they're mine, that's the way you wanted it, isn't it, pet? Wherever you are, poor Allen, it's going to be just as you wanted it for me, everything I've ever dreamed of at my fingertips . . .

After a time she stood up, her legs and arms tingling with relief and excitement. Carefully she fed the diamonds into the pouch again, tightened the drawstring at the top. She found one of her bras and put it on and then tucked the pouch between her breasts. It was like a lover's hand, like Allen's hand, caressing her.

Now that she had the diamonds, the despair and the feeling of being trapped were gone. She felt euphoric, lightheaded, as if she were mildly drunk. She wanted to be free of this hellish place, to get back to civilization, and yet there was no longer any urgency. She could leave right away . . . but there were only a couple of hours of daylight left now, and cars on these backcountry roads were sure to be few and far between in the evening. And the last thing she ought to be doing was walking alone in strange surroundings after dark, carrying the diamonds.

Wouldn't it be better to spend another night here? After all this time she had nothing to fear; and she could pack a few things in one of the suitcases and then fix herself something to eat, she hadn't eaten anything all day and she was suddenly quite hungry. In the morning, refreshed, with her hair combed and her makeup in place, she could walk away from here before it got too hot, all the way to Puerto Pollensa if necessary. A ride into Palma, a place to stay, a job or a man who would pay her for the use of her body . . . all the while guarding the diamonds until she could save enough for plane fare to England. Once she was in London she would find a way to sell the diamonds, all but one, which she would have made into a ring, a memento of Allen. Then another man, the right one this time, a rich one to marry a rich woman, and her future would be secure.

Lord, how lovely it was all going to be at last!

TUESDAY EVENING – CARMODY

He stood on the balcony of his villa, smoking one of his short, thin cigars, watching a red sun low over the Mediterranean that was like a round spot of blood leaking crimson shadows into the sky around it. His lips were thinned into a razorlike slash. His thoughts smoldered darkly.

He had been back on Majorca just over an hour, home for fifteen minutes. At first inspection it had appeared as if no one had been inside the villa since he had closed it up on Saturday. But on closer inspection there were small signs of intrusion: a few inches missing from his bottle of Johnnie Walker Black Label, rarely used; faint scratch marks on the balcony door lock; tiny particles of broken glass on the balcony floor. And out here, too, the residue of bloodstains that somebody hadn't quite cleaned up.

Someone—probably Allen Fanning—had been killed

184

here. In his home. *In his home!*

Miralles was going to pay and pay dearly for that. Using a man's house for an act of violence was in itself an act of violence, a kind of rape. It couldn't be forgotten or condoned. It had to be avenged.

Even so, and even though this had been his base of operations for the past few years, he was going to have to give it up — find some other place to live on Majorca or in Spain or maybe in another part of Europe. Not because the villa had been violated; because too many people knew about it now. That was plain enough. He wouldn't have had this trouble with Miralles and Alvarez if his home base was a more closely guarded secret. He liked this place as much as he could ever like any place, but there were other villas, and the area didn't matter much to him, as long as it wasn't Málaga or Torremolinos. And when he moved, nobody was going to be told his new location. He never made the same mistake twice if he could help it.

From inside he heard the burr of the telephone. He had made a call to Majorca from the airport in Málaga and it was time for a response; he hurried in and caught up the receiver. "Yes?"

It wasn't the man he'd called from Málaga. But the voice was familiar; it said, "Ah, Señor Carmody, you are home — good. This is Pepé, in Palma Nova."

Pepé, in Palma Nova, was Pepé Vallori, owner of Pepé's Spanish Bar. He was trustworthy; he took messages and looked after the villa when Carmody was away from the island. But he was still one more person who knew the villa's location, one of too many.

"What is it, Pepé?"

"A young woman, Señor Carmody. She came here alone a few hours ago and asked if I would contact you. She claims to know you and that her business with you is most urgent."

"Yes? She have a name?"

"*Sí, amigo.* Gillian Waltham."

"She still there?"

"Sí. She is afraid, Señor Carmody, of that I am certain. That is why I agreed to call you. This is the third time I have tried."

"Put her on the phone."

There was thirty seconds of silence; then Gillian's voice said, "Oh, Mr. Carmody, thank God. I've got to talk to you—right away. Please, it's important."

Now it was *Mister* Carmody. He said, "Yes? What do you want?"

"Not on the phone. Can't we meet? Here or wherever you say?"

"Suppose you come out to my place. Or do you have objections to that?"

"No, no, anywhere you say."

"Give me Pepé again." She put the bar owner back on the line and Carmody said to him, "You sure she came alone? Nobody else hanging around since she's been there?"

"I am sure she is alone, *amigo.*"

"Put her in a taxi, then, and send her out here. Don't waste any time. I expect to be going out pretty soon."

He hung up, poured himself a small Veterano cognac, sat with it in one of the heavy leather chairs. Twenty minutes crept away; the phone stayed silent. The sound of a car coming into the clearing in front brought him out of the chair. He drew the Beretta, peered through the louvered shutters across a front window. One of the gray Seats that served as taxis in Palma Nova had pulled up behind his Porsche 911-T Targa, and Gillian was just climbing out. She was alone.

Carmody watched her come to the door, the taxi U-turn and start back down the hill. The bell was ringing. He went and opened the door. She started to say something when she saw him, but he caught her arm, pulled her inside, shut and locked the door again.

She was nervous-eyed, her mouth pinched, her face pale. She looked at the gun as if it were a live cobra he was holding, with a mixture of fear and fascination.

He put the Beretta away; he didn't see the need to scare her any more than she already was. "All right," he said, "tell me what it is you want."

"I . . . it's about . . . about Zaanhof."

"What about Zaanhof?"

"He . . . he's dead."

"Yes? How did he die? Did you kill him?"

"No! I mean . . . I hit him, yes, with a wood statue. He tried to attack me and I defended myself and he fell and the back of his head hit a table . . . God, it was awful . . ."

"Why didn't you tell me this this morning? Why did you lie to me?"

"I was afraid. And I couldn't remember where his villa was, you have to believe that. It's somewhere in Málaga but I—"

"Why did you come to Majorca?" Carmody asked her. "Just to tell me you'd lied about Zaanhof?"

"No. I lost my bracelet at the villa, I didn't realize it until after you left Liane's this morning. It has my name on it. If the police find it . . . or the man who paid Zaanhof . . . they'll think I *murdered* him. They'll come after me . . . oh God, I need your help, that's why I'm here."

"My help to do what?"

"Get me out of Spain. I know it's crazy but . . . that's what you do, isn't it? Help people in my kind of trouble? I don't have any money but I can do something to pay you . . . anything . . ."

"Two days ago you hated my guts, this morning you were petrified of me, and now you're willing to sleep with me in exchange for my help. You're a piece of work, you are. You go through feelings for people like a kid through a bag of candy."

"Please, you don't understand—"

"I understand just fine," Carmody said. "You lost your bracelet and you're worried about the police. It's too bad you didn't think to look through Zaanhof's wallet. If you had, you'd have found the two thousand dollars he owed you and you could be on your way back to the States by now, free and clear."

She stared at him open-mouthed. "You . . . how did you—?"

The telphone rang.

Carmody turned away from her, went to answer the call. This was the one he'd been expecting—from a Mallorquina named Ibañez, who did some work for him now and then on the island. Ibañez said, "He is at the Hotel Mallorca Grande, Señor Carmody. The presidential suite."

"Staff with him? Bodyguards?"

"No one. He came alone."

"Good. That makes things easier."

"But you should be careful anyway," Ibañez said. "Carlos Miralles is a dangerous man."

"Somebody should have told him the same thing about me," Carmody said. He put the receiver down, turned to Gillian again. "I've got things to do. Your time's up."

"Oh, but you can't just . . . the money, my bracelet . . ."

"Right, the money and your bracelet."

He took out his wallet, removed the two thousand dollars in fifties and hundreds, pressed the money into her hands. Then he dipped her silver bracelet from his jacket pocket and dropped it on top of the bills.

She gaped at the pile in disbelief. All she managed to say was, "Oh!"

Carmody said, "You can stop worrying about the police now; they don't even know you exist. Go the hell home where you belong."

"But . . . but I—"

"I don't have time to run a taxi service," he said. "Call yourself a cab unless you want to walk back to Palma Nova. And make sure the door is locked when you leave." He started out of the room, into the front hallway.

"Wait!" Gillian called after him. "You can't just go away without explaining—"

He went through the door and shut it behind him,

chopping off the rest of her words. He slid into the Porsche. By the time he'd driven halfway down the access road, he had forgotten about Gillian Waltham. He was thinking about Carlos Miralles.

TUESDAY EVENING — GILLIAN

Alone in the heavy silence, Gillian kept looking at the silver bracelet and the two thousand dollars cupped in her hands. She was still having difficulty believing it. The two things she'd wanted most and thought she'd never see again, just like that. Her safety, her life in her own hands again, just like that. The relief that surged through her was so intense it was almost sexual.

She returned to the living room, sat on the heavy sofa. Carmody must have found Zaanhof's villa somehow, gotten there before anyone else. Found Zaanhof, dead, and her bracelet, and realized what had happened. But what she couldn't understand was why he'd taken the bracelet and the money and given them to her without asking anything in return. A man like him, a hard man who didn't seem to care about anybody except himself . . . why?

Then she thought: What difference does it make why

he did it? He did it, that's what matters. And now I'm free of him and men like him, I never have to set eyes on him again. Just call a cab, take it all the way into Palma, spend the night at a *pensión,* and make airline reservations in the morning. Palma to Madrid, Madrid to New York, New York to Cleveland, Cleveland to Canton . . . I'll be home in two days.

But she didn't get up and go to the phone; she kept on sitting there. Thinking about Carmody, thinking that it *did* make a difference why he'd done it. *You go through feelings for people like a kid through a bag of candy.* Well, maybe so where he was concerned. Right now what she felt for him was a bewildered gratitude—she really did want to know why he'd helped her. Should she stay until he got back, ask him why, try to thank him? Another crazy idea, Gil. The one that had brought her to Majorca had worked out fine, but one crazy idea ought to be anybody's limit. He hadn't said when he would be back; he might be away all night, or days. And if she was here when he returned, he'd probably mistake her intentions. He'd probably expect her to show him how grateful she was by going to bed with him, and she wasn't going to do that. No way was she going to do that.

She wondered what it would be like.

The thought both repulsed and excited her. She wasn't going to do it, she was ashamed of herself for even thinking about it, but she couldn't get the curiosity out of her mind. Would he be a rough lover, caring only about himself and his pleasure? Or would he be surprisingly gentle and considerate? A hard exterior didn't necessarily mean—

"No," she said aloud. "Don't be a damn fool. Haven't you been a damn fool enough times already in the past year?"

She put the money in her purse, the bracelet on her left wrist. When she stood her gaze fell on the portable bar across the room. She could use a drink, she thought; the emotional roller coaster she'd spent the day riding was taking its toll. Would Carmody mind? A small cognac? No, he wouldn't mind; then she'd call for a taxi. She started over to the bar.

From outside, below and to one side of the balcony, something made a sharp scraping sound.

Gillian stopped, listening. The scraping sound came again, and again; then there was the clicking of dislodged pebbles rolling down an incline. An animal, she told herself, some kind of animal—but now there was a coldness on the back of her neck.

Hesitantly she went to the balcony doors and peered out and saw nothing. But more rocks tumbled, it sounded as though they were rolling directly beneath the balcony, and on impulse she opened the doors and stepped out cautiously until she was almost to the far railing. She craned her neck forward to look down at the rocky slope below.

Somebody was down there—a man, picking his way along the fall with his body hunched and eyes searching the ground.

Gillian stood motionless, watching as the man straightened and began to make his way laterally across the incline. The setting sun hung in a purple-streaked sky now, its light golden, and where the light filtered through and above the pines it touched portions of the slanting ground. When the man stepped out of shadow into one of those golden patches, his face was clearly distinguishable in three-quarter profile.

The breath she'd been holding exploded out of Gillian no less violently than if she'd been punched in the stomach. For the second time in half an hour she felt stunned and incredulous—because she knew him. She knew him as intimately as any woman can know any man.

He was the lover she'd thought she loved, the lover whose love had been a lie.

He was Fernando Marí.

TUESDAY EVENING – SILVERA

There was nothing on the slope, as Silvera had known would be the case. But he moved back and forth across it, as he had yesterday morning, until he reached the spot where the pines took over. Then he paused to look to where he had buried Allen Fanning in the shallow grave.

No. He would not uncover the corpse. There was nothing left in the clothing, he had emptied all the pockets; he could not possibly have missed an item as large as a leatherbound notebook. Digging up the body would be a waste of time. And time was a factor now, because he didn't know how soon Carmody would return and he wanted to be finished with this fool's errand quickly.

He knew Carmody had come back to Majorca because he had seen him only a few minutes ago. He had been on foot, making his way upward through the trees that bordered the access road, when he heard the roar of the Porsche's engine. A few seconds later the car had sped by dustily. The driver was Carmody. Silvera had seen the American once, years ago in Madrid; there was no mistaking that lean, hard face.

He had thought then, as he did again now, that a confrontation with a man such as Carmody was to be avoided if at all possible. The *patrón* was an old fool if he thought otherwise. Silvera was not afraid of Carmody, but a wise man did not kill those with power and influence except as a last resort; it was likely to bring the wrath of others down upon his head. This was why he had swallowed his anger at the *patrón's* insults and threats. If a lesser man had dared to speak to him that way, Silvera would have cut his throat; he was no peasant, no son of a whore. It would be a pleasure to spill the *patrón's* bright red blood . . . but it would be just as much a pleasure to continue spending his bright green money. And much, much safer.

Silvera climbed the slope again, pulled himself onto the stone wall at the top, climbed up onto the balcony. There would be nothing here either—hadn't he cleaned up all traces before leaving yesterday morning? But he would satisfy himself and the *patrón* that Fanning's secretary had not been overlooked.

He crossed first to the glass doors, looked inside briefly, then began to prowl the balcony. Its floor, its railings were empty. All that was left was the stone barbecue; he turned to that, poked among the stones, lifted the grate, used a pair of tongs to sift through the ashes.

One of the tongs struck something that was not a piece of charcoal. Silvera prodded it up to where he could see it.

Rectangular, made of leather—a notebook.

He lifted it out with the tongs, blew away the fine gray ash that coated it. There was surprise in him, that he had been wrong and the *patrón* had been right, but nothing more; it was not in his makeup to be self-critical. Carefully he opened the secretary. Inside were several folded slips of paper, a memo calendar with events and reminders in a precise hand, and an alphabetized index of names, addresses, telephone numbers.

Silvera flipped through the names first. There was no listing for Jennifer Evans. The folded slips of paper next — and the third one he opened was a rental receipt from a Palma *immobilia*. It was made out to Jennifer Evans, for a week's rental of a Farm Xorrigo in the interior of the island, with the village of Santa Margarita as its postal address; and it was dated six days ago.

A smile formed on Silvera's mouth as he closed the notebook, slipped it into his pocket. If she was still waiting at this farm, Fanning's Jennifer Evans, if she had the diamonds or could be made to tell him where they were, this would be a good day after all for Diego Silvera. The best kind of day — one filled with bright green money *and* bright red blood.

TUESDAY EVENING — JENNIFER

In the master bedroom, she stood at one of the shuttered windows overlooking the balcony, peering through
the louvers, watching Fernando Marí take something from
inside the barbecue. She couldn't tell what it was, or what
he was doing with it; his back was to her and his head
was tilted downward over the object. What was it and why
had it been in the barbecue? Why was *he* here? What
connection did Fernando have with Carmody?

The questions, along with a dozen others, tumbled
through her mind. Fernando . . . he had told her he was
a businessman, an importer-exporter who did a lot of
traveling, but that must have been a lie, too, like his other
lies . . . Zaanhof saying he'd heard about her, about her
acting abilities, from "a mutual friend"—of course, she
should have realized it must be Fernando . . . Zaanhof,
Fernando, Carmody, all mixed up together . . . that was
why Fernando was here, something to do with the trick

against Carmody and the man who had ordered it—Fernando's boss as well as Zaanhof's?

What if he came inside? What if he found her here?

Carmody hadn't hurt her, but Fernando—would *he* hurt her?

So tender when they'd made love, except for that last time, when he'd put his hands on her throat and squeezed so hard while he was climaxing. She'd had to fight free and he'd apologized, but his face . . . that look on his face while he was squeezing her throat . . .

The memory made her shudder. God, what kind of man was underneath that handsome charm? Not just a shallow, self-indulgent one. And not a harmless one. Dangerous. Even more dangerous than Carmody . . .

He mustn't know she was in the house. Thank God she'd had enough sense not to call out to him from the balcony; to step back inside and quietly shut the balcony doors and come in here. There was no telling what he might do if he found her here.

She watched him turn away from the railing, put the object he'd found into his coat pocket—something that looked like a leather book of some kind. He was smiling now, a smile Gillian had never seen on him before: ugly, primitive. Obscene.

I gave myself to him, I let him inside my body, I loved him.

She took an involuntary step back from the window, feeling suddenly unclean. The heel of her shoe caught on something, and when she twisted away from it reflexively she saw—too late—that it was an electrical cord attached to a lamp on the bedside table.

The lamp seemed to come flying toward her. She clutched frantically at it but she couldn't hold it; it hit the floor, rolled against the wall. The sound it made was not loud, but it was too loud just the same. In her ears it was like a thunderclap.

She ran across to the door, flung it open—and he was just coming through the balcony doors. There was a gun in his hand, a *gun!* A scream tore out of her throat; she tried to run away from him into the front hallway. He caught her before she'd taken more than a few steps, spun her around, and she cried, "Fernando!" in a pleading voice. She had no time to say anything else. He didn't hesitate for even a second.

The last thing she saw was the gun barrel coming toward her face in a vicious arc .

TUESDAY,
LATE EVENING — CARMODY

When the lean, gray-haired man opened the door and looked out at him irritably, Carmody showed him the Beretta and said, "Back up, Miralles, and don't do anything to make me kill you before we talk."

Carlos Miralles stared at the gun, his face impassive, his body rigid. Then, slowly, his eyes lifted to Carmody's face—bright eyes that contained fury but no fear. "What do you want here with your gun, eh?"

"Back up, like I told you," Carmody said. "Do it!"

Miralles obeyed, in stiff, slow movements. When he was five feet from the door Carmody stepped inside and shut it behind him. "Keep going," he said, and Miralles continued to back up until he was standing in the middle of his lavishly furnished suite, the best the Hotel Mallorca Grande had to offer.

"You know my name," Miralles said. "Do you know who I am?"

"I know, all right. You're a stupid son of a bitch who thinks everybody falls on his knees when you point your finger. But I don't fall, Miralles. And I don't scare. You know who *I* am?"

Hot blood had darkened the old man's face. He said, "Carmody."

"That's right, Carmody. I know some other things, too. All about the diamonds Allen Fanning stole from you, and how you set me up to get them back."

"How do you know?"

"That's nothing for you."

Miralles' teeth were bared now, like an animal showing its fangs. "You have *cojones*, Señor Carmody, to come here with your gun, to talk to me as you have. I respect men with *cojones*—but I do not like being threatened."

"No? Well, I don't like being played for a sucker, or having my home used for a death trap. The hell with your reasons; they don't matter to me. You owe me now, Miralles, that's what matters. If I don't collect one way or another I don't stay in business. So I intend to collect."

"Leave here with your gun, now, and you will be well paid. This I promise you."

"How well paid?"

"Another five thousand dollars."

"Not enough. Not even close to being enough."

"Then what is your price?"

"Another twenty-five thousand."

"Hah!" The sound was a bullish snort, not a laugh. Miralles was making a visible effort to control himself. "No man's trouble is worth that much money to me. You will take another five thousand, and we will forget this invasion of my privacy, we will forget your insolent threats; we will not bother each other again."

"You think it's as simple as that?" Carmody said. "Not hardly. The more you fuck around, Miralles, the more it's going to cost you."

"I will not be intimidated! I have killed men with my own hands for milder words than you speak."

"Yes? Well, I'm the one with the gun."

"Your gun means nothing to me," Miralles said. "Are you such an oaf to think you can kill me in this room, this fine hotel, and expect to walk away a free man?"

"There are other places, other times—I can get to you, Miralles, even in that fancy *palacio* of yours in Torremolinos. Or I can arrange for somebody else to get to you. I mean what I say. Believe it."

Miralles was shaking; it was like watching a pot about to boil over. "*Qué te la mame tu madre!*" he shouted. "I will not stand for your extortion! I will not stand for it!"

"Thirty thousand," Carmody said flatly. "Deposited in my Swiss bank within three days."

"In three days you will be dead! A hundred men will fight one another for the privilege of killing you to please Miralles!"

"The people I deal with are professionals, not a bunch of half-assed punks working for a little tin god. I can disappear in a few hours, Miralles, so completely that you couldn't find me with ten thousand men. Be smart, pay the money. And don't even think of trying any bullshit doublecross afterward. You're in over your head this time and I'm letting you off easy. Think about it."

"I think about nothing! *Estó me jóde!*"

Miralles took two steps forward, hands fisted; his face was the color of raw liver. Carmody set himself with the gun drawn back, ready to use it as a club if Miralles jumped him. But the old man stopped suddenly, stiffening. His eyes bulged, his mouth twisted into a rictus of pain. A hoarse, strangled sound rattled in his throat. One hand came up and clawed at his chest, as if he were scratching himself—and then he went to his knees, hard and gracelessly, like a fighting bull spine-pricked by a *descabello* after an unsuccessful matador kill. He knelt there, staring up at Carmody open-mouthed for several seconds, gasping; then he pitched sideways and rolled onto his back.

Heart attack, Carmody thought. For Christ's sake!

TUESDAY NIGHT – SILVERA

There was a map of the island in the rented Seat's glove compartment, and Silvera drove with it spread open on the seat beside him. From Calvia he took the switchbacked road over the mountains to the junction with the Palma-Esporlas road, then maneuvered over unpaved country lanes until he came to Santa María. There he joined one of the main two-lane roads, skirted Majorca's second largest city, Inca, and approached the village of Santa Margarita.

Thinking about what would happen when he reached Farm Xorrigo, he felt excitement build hotly in his loins. The gods were being good to him tonight. Jennifer Evans . . . and Gillian Waltham, too. He glanced into the rear seat; Gillian was still motionless under the blanket. He had hit her again, after leaving Calvia, to make certain she stayed unconscious until it was time for her to wake up for him.

Gillian. He had been truly amazed when she cried his

name, when he recognized her. Why she had been at
Carmody's villa was a puzzle to him—but he did not really
care to know the reason. Her fate was sealed in any case,
the poor stupid American *coño*. She had seen him, she
knew him, she would have to die too tonight. He remembered her body, the feel of her tight and wet around him;
the fires burned hotter, his palms were damp; he knew
just what he would do to her. First Jennifer Evans and
then Gillian, two in one night, two in one night . . .

Silvera realized how rapidly he was breathing, felt the
hard ache of his arousal, and understood that he must
control himself. The pleasure would come later; first he
must make sure, this time, that he recovered the diamonds.
The *patrón* would not settle for less, and like it or not,
he must make the *patrón* happy to preserve his own
happiness.

The old man was still in a rage. Silvera had stopped
briefly in Calvia, a few kilometers from Carmody's villa,
and charmed the woman owner of an *especiería* into letting
him use her telephone. He had decided it would be best
to call the *patrón*, let him know that he had been right
and the notebook had been found; it would smooth the
old vulture's ruffled feathers, he had reasoned. But no, the
response to his news had been angry grunts and the
receiver slammed down in his ear. Hostile, obsessed *carajo*!
He would be satisfied only when his precious diamonds
were safely in his hands.

It was dark, the rising moon pale in the sky, when
Silvera reached Santa Margarita. He passed through the
semi-deserted village, found the correct secondary road,
began to follow its twisting path through forestland and
farmland. The map was one of the comprehensive types,
put out by the provincial government, that gave the location of each farm; the one labeled Xorrigo was the eighth
out from the village, but none of the entry lanes or rural
mailboxes was marked. He slowed his speed radically,
to make certain he didn't miscount by overlooking a
track or a farmhouse hidden behind trees or one of the

crumbling stone walls.

When he finally located Xorrigo, there was nothing to see except a narrow rocky lane winding through a copse of pine; the farm buildings were invisible from the road. Silvera shut off his headlamps, turned onto the lane between two stone cairns and inched along to minimize engine noise. He was three-quarters of the way through the pines before he could see the farmhouse and grounds ahead. He stopped at that point, switched off the ignition.

On the back seat, Gillian was starting to stir, her breathing becoming irregular. Silvera leaned over the seat, pulled the blanket away and smiled tenderly at her bruised face. "No, *querida,* not yet," he said, and hit her with bunched fingers along the jaw—hard but not as hard as he would later, and not yet with the quartz ring. She stopped stirring, lay motionless again.

He got out of the car, latching the door quietly, and walked along the track until he reached the edge of the red-earth farmyard. There was a light in the crumbling old house, shining through the strands of beads that served in place of a front door. His smile reappeared. Jennifer Evans was still here, of a certainty. And that meant the diamonds were still here too.

It was unlikely that she would be watching outside, but she would be wary after her long wait and she might have a weapon. He must be wary too. His gaze swept over the yard, the stone outbuildings, the livestock corrals, the fenced section of prickly pear that grew like an elongated extention of the house on one side. It reminded him of the poor village of Esteban de Bao where he had spent his boyhood, and the memory was unpleasant; he shunted it out of his mind.

He moved laterally through the trees until he was opposite the first of the outbuildings. Then he came out and circled behind the building, past a well, to the patch of cactus. When he paused to listen there he could hear the faint rattle of dishes inside the house. Eating her supper, perhaps. He laughed silently. Her last supper.

As he passed under the grape arbor, he drew his friend the Browning automatic. Dishes still rattled within, and now he could hear the hollow click of footsteps on floor tiles. He went to the beaded doorway, stepped out with his left hand braced against the wall, and looked around and through the beads, inside.

At first he saw nothing—a sparsely furnished room, disarranged as if it had been ransacked. Then, through an archway, the woman moved into view in an ancient, lanternlit kitchen. Tall, blonde, attractive, wearing only a brassiere . . . a fact that made her lean nakedness all the more exciting. Better and better, Silvera thought, smiling. It was always so much more enjoyable when the woman was pretty, soft and warm and pretty.

He waited until she stopped moving, stood framed beyond the archway. Then he stepped through the glass beads to introduce himself: Diego Silvera, the man who was going to take her life.

TUESDAY NIGHT – JENNIFER

She heard the beads clicking, swung around and gaped at the man coming through the doorway . . . a stranger, a smiling stranger with a gun in his hand. The plate of cheese she had been carrying slipped out of her fingers, shattered on the floor. There was a cry in her throat, but it was caught there, like a bone that she couldn't dislodge. She couldn't seem to move, either; shock had turned her legs into blocks of stone.

The man stopped a few paces from her, holding the gun up in front of her face, smiling broadly, and as soon as Jennifer saw his eyes she knew she was going to die. The knowledge was utterly alien. Her stomach convulsed, her groin felt as if a hand were brutally clutching her there. Her throat unlocked and she heard herself say in a shrill, cracking voice, "Who are you, what do you want?"

"I am Diego Silvera," he said. "It is you I want, *querida*. You—and the diamonds."

Her terror was raw and wild, but she felt a savage bitterness, too. The diamonds, *her* diamonds . . . so close to having everything and now she would have nothing, nothing . . . "No!" she screamed at him, taking a step backward, her hands lifting protectively to her breast. "No, they're mine, I won't let you have them!"

He moved as swiftly as a striking snake. Hit her with the palm of his free hand, then backhanded her and cut her cheek with his ring. She cried out, put a hand up to her bleeding cheek—and his fingers caught the front of her brassiere and ripped powerfully downward. The bra snaps broke, baring her breasts; the chamois pouch full of diamonds dropped to the floor at her feet.

Jennifer went to her knees after it, clutching at the pouch, and Silvera kicked her, kicked her again, breathing hard but not with exertion. She sprawled backward into the kitchen table, upsetting it, bringing dishes and battered silverware down around her. She was on her knees, whimpering, her mind a cauldron of pain and fear. One of her hands touched something . . . cold, hard . . . and when she looked at it she saw that it was a knife, the one she had been about to use to slice the cheese.

Her fingers closed over it, he wouldn't get her diamonds, she would kill him! He was on his haunches now, still smiling, filthy shit, picking up the chamois pouch, his eyes on it and not her; she stumbled up and ran at him with the knife upraised. But he heard her, saw her before she reached him. The smile vanished and he threw himself to one side as she slashed down at his head, missing it, carving nothing but air.

In the same instant the gun in his hand made a thunderous noise and there was sudden agony in her chest, a great burning. She dropped the knife, stared down at the raw wound where her right breast had been.

Look what he did to me, she thought in awe.

And then she died.

TUESDAY NIGHT — SILVERA

The dead Jennifer Evans made him even angrier than the live one had. He kicked her petulantly, like a child deprived of a special treat. *Puta*, he thought, *puta*, why did you make me do that? I didn't want to kill you that way!

But she had surprised him, coming at him with a knife that way, and his finger tightening on the Browning's trigger had been reflexive. If he had kept his eyes on her, it would not have happened; he would have seen her pick up the knife, he would have had time to take it away from her. Now it was too late. Now she was dead, too fast, too fast, and with hardly any blood.

He stood cursing her, loudly, until his anger spent itself. Then he remembered Gillian, waiting for him in the car. And all at once he was smiling again.

The Evans woman was dead, yes, but nothing else had changed. He had the diamonds, he had Gillian, he had as much time as he cared to take with *her*, and later tonight he would have the *patrón's* money. He felt the power rising in him again, the pleasure fires rekindling. Gillian. Yes, yes, Gillian . . .

Silvera picked up the pouch, opened it to make certain it contained all the stolen diamonds, then pocketed it. Still holding the Browning, he went out through the glass beads. The moon was higher now, brighter, and the dusty air was warm and caressing, woman-soft, against his face. He began to hurry, smiling, thinking of Gillian.

He was halfway across the farmyard when Carmody came out from under the grape arbor and shot him twice in the upper body.

TUESDAY NIGHT – CARMODY

Carlos Miralles wasn't dead—not yet, anyway. He lay on his back on the Hotel Mallorca Grande's expensive carpet, his stomach convulsing, making labored gasping sounds as he fought for breath. His face was a livid purple.

Carmody said, "I ought to let you die, you son of a bitch." Instead he went to one knee beside the stricken Spaniard, searched through his clothing without finding any pharmaceuticals. Swearing softly, he hurried into the bedroom. In a toilet kit he found a vial of nitroglycerin tablets, with instructions in Spanish on the label. He took them back to where Miralles lay making the strangling sounds, the whites of his eyes showing now. Carmody fished out a tablet, wedged it under Miralles' tongue. He didn't wait to see if it would do any good; he straightened and went to the telephone to call the hotel doctor.

It rang just as he put his hand on it.

Carmody hesitated. Then, when the bell rang again,

he picked up the phone and carried it on its long cord into the bedroom and shut the door, so the caller couldn't hear the sounds Miralles was making. He lifted the receiver, made a deep, guttural acknowledgment as Miralles might have done it.

A man's soft voice said, *"Patrón?"* Carmody grunted again, and the man seemed to take him for Miralles, all right, because he launched into a short monologue in Spanish. Carmody understood most of it: an apology for some disagreement he and Miralles had had earlier tonight; something about Miralles being right about the notebook, he'd found it at Carmody's villa after all; and then: "Fanning's woman is at Farm Xorrigo near the village of Santa Margarita. I am on my way there now, *patrón*. If she is still at the farm, you will have your diamonds before midnight—this I promise you."

Carmody's hand was so tight around the receiver there was pain the length of his arm. He wanted to say something, tell this man, this hired gun, to come to the hotel instead; but his Spanish wasn't nearly good enough. All he could do was make another grunting sound, slam the receiver down hard—and hope the hired gun took it to mean Miralles was still pissed at him.

He went out into the sitting room. Miralles was still alive, still strangling, but his color was better; maybe he would die and maybe he wouldn't. Carmody didn't give a damn either way, except that with the old bugger dead there wouldn't be any payoff for him. Unless he got to the diamonds first.

He lifted the receiver again, jiggled the cradle bar. When the hotel operator came on, Carmody said, "Carlos Miralles has had a heart attack. Send a doctor up right away." He didn't wait for a response. He put the phone down and let himself out of the room. There was a stairwell at the near end of the corridor; he went down that way, through the bar and out a side entrance.

In his Porsche he checked his comprehensive island map, located Santa Margarita and Farm Xorrigo. As he drove swiftly away from the hotel, through El Terreno, he focused his anger on the faceless, soft-voiced man who murdered people for Carlos Miralles. Whoever he was, he'd killed Allen Fanning at Carmody's villa and he'd gone back there tonight . . . and found Gillian, killed her too? Or had she left by the time the hired gun got there? He told himself it didn't really matter, Gillian was nothing to him, but he couldn't stop thinking about her, wondering if she was all right. He didn't like the idea, but for the first time in his life a woman other than Chana had got down inside him . . .

When he reached the outskirts of Palma he pushed the Porsche as much as he dared on the two-lane blacktop leading to Inca and the northeast coast, alert for Guardia Civil motorcycle patrols. It took him forty-five minutes to get to Santa Margarita, another fifteen minutes to find the entrance to Farm Xorrigo. He parked in the trees across from the entry lane, went with the Beretta in hand up the lane between the stone cairns. At the start of the pines, he stepped off into the trees and made his way through them, keeping the road in sight.

When he saw the dark shape of the Seat he stopped and swore under his breath. The hired gun had apparently gotten here first. He listened, heard no sounds from the car, and approached it through the trees. Went in a crouch to the driver's side, then raised up to peer through the windows.

The front seat was empty, but there was a mound of something under a blanket in the rear. Carmody's lips pulled away from his teeth. The back door was unlocked; he opened it slowly, watching for a dome light. None came on. He leaned in and dragged the blanket away.

Gillian. At first he thought she was dead, but when he put a hand between her breasts he could feel the irregular thump of her heart. Relief moved through him—a deeper relief than he wanted to acknowledge. When he touched her face he could feel cuts, dried blood. The son of a bitch had abused her . . . but why he'd brought her with him, left her alive this long, Carmody couldn't figure. He tugged her toward him, lifted her inert weight out of the car. The road ahead, the farmyard in the distance, appeared deserted. Even so, he didn't like the idea of restricting the freedom of his hands; but he didn't want to hang around the car and he didn't want to leave her inside it.

He carried her into the pines, out of sight of the road, then put her down. Her hands and feet were tied; he cut the cords with his knife, then knelt and chafed her wrists, slapped her face gently. Her eyelids fluttered and she began to moan softly. Carmody covered her mouth with his hand. Her eyes opened wide; he could feel the sudden straining tenseness of her body. He whispered, "It's all right, it's Carmody, you're safe now."

Her body went limp. He took his hand away from her mouth—and she struggled into a sitting positon and threw her arms around him, saying breathlessly, "Oh God, he came into the villa, he hit me, he—"

Carmody said, "Save it," and pulled her arms down. "There's no time for that now."

She looked around, confused, disoriented. "Where are we? Where's Fernando? How did you—?"

"Never mind, I said. Can you walk?"

"I . . . I think so." Then, "He hurt me . . . my face hurts."

"Come on, on your feet. And don't ask questions; just do what I tell you."

He lifted her up, led her back toward the Seat. At the edge of the road he stopped to reconnoiter. Still nobody around. He pressed the keys to the Porsche into her hand.

"Follow this track until you come out on the road," he said. "My Porsche is parked in the trees on the other side. Get in and lock the doors and put the keys in the ignition. You know how to drive a standard transmission?"

"Yes."

"If anybody comes out of here but me, start the car and go away fast. We're at Farm Xorrigo, near Santa Margarita. There's a map in the glove box to show you how to get back to Palma Nova. Go to Pepé's and wait there. Clear?"

"I . . . yes. But what about—?"

"No questions. Move."

She nodded, went away unsteadily through the trees. Carmody returned to the Seat, jerked wires loose under the dash. That done, he ran ahead toward the farmhouse.

He heard the shrill cry of a woman just as he came in sight of it. She was shouting something, the words indistinguishable. Carmody took a moment to study the house, the farmyard, before going to the far end of the clearing. There were more sounds now, something falling, something shattering; seconds later a gun went off, hollowly, a single report. After that, he heard only silence.

He left the woods, ran through deep shadow until he reached the grape arbor. He hunkered down behind a rusting metal swing, watching the house with his flat gaze. Less than a minute had passed when the glass beads in the doorway tinkled and the man, Miralles' hired gun, came out into the yard.

The moonlight was bright enough for Carmody to see the automatic held loosely in the tall Spaniard's hand. He didn't hesitate; there was a big score to settle here. He rose up and stepped out from under the arbor and squeezed off twice with the Beretta.

TUESDAY NIGHT – SILVERA

The impact of the bullets knocked Silvera down. But they didn't keep him down where he fell, didn't numb his mind the way they did the right side of his chest. Almost immediately he rolled and scrambled on elbows and knees toward the nearest of the stone fences. Myrtle and evergreen shrubs grew in close to the fence, forming pockets of deep shadow; he dragged himself into one of these just as a spray of dirt washed over his right leg and the gun sounded again behind him.

The Browning was still in his grasp; he twisted around with it, tried to find Carmody in the moonlit darkness and did not see him anywhere. He was sure it was Carmody, even though he hadn't gotten a look at the one who'd shot him. It made no sense that he was here; how could he have found Farm Xorrigo so soon after Silvera himself had learned of its existence? And yet it could not be anybody else. Jennifer Evans had been alone, he was certain of that;

215

and the Guardia Civil would have come with a dozen men and lights and they would not have shot him without warning. Carmody, only Carmody . . . and now he would kill the man, gladly. Now it was not only a necessity, it would be a pleasure to cut his belly open and empty his entrails on the ground and grind them under his foot.

Something moved near the farmhouse, at the remains of an old wooden cart. Silvera raised the Browning, fired once, and the movement stopped. Without hesitation he scuttled backward several feet because the muzzle flash would have betrayed his position. His body was still in motion when he saw the flash of light from the farmhouse wall, heard the bullet slap the earth where he had been lying and then the rolling echo of the shot. He fired in turn at the place where he had seen the light, drew farther back along the fence. This time there was no answering shot. But he didn't believe he had hit Carmody; he would not fall for any such ploy as that.

The activity had caused pain to erupt through the numbness in his chest. Silvera explored the wounds with his fingertips, grimacing. The one below his collarbone was the worst; the bullet must have severed nerves or muscles, for he could barely move his arm. It and the wound lower down, along his rib cage, were bleeding profusely. He did not like the feel of his own blood. It enraged him, made him sick to his stomach. He would have to have a doctor—and soon, very soon. Before the bleeding made him too weak to travel.

He looked up at the night sky, to where the moon sat fat and white above the hilltops. Its light was both good and bad: he could see Carmody if he left cover, but Carmody could also see him. And he could not afford to play a waiting game because of his wounds.

He would have to be bold, then, force Carmody into making a mistake that would leave him vulnerable. He would have to find an edge.

TUESDAY NIGHT – CARMODY

Carmody lay belly-down along the side of the farmhouse and cursed himself for not making killing shots with
his first two rounds. He'd had the element of surprise on
his side; he'd been only ten yards from the Spaniard; and
he'd had the moonlight to aim by. A kid with a .22 could
have put a round through the hired gun's eye at that range,
with that much light—and yet he'd missed the heart not
once but twice.

So far he hadn't done any of it right. He'd let his
emotions get in the way like a frigging amateur. And when
he'd seen the hired gun sliding along the ground and pulled
up and steadied himself for the third shot, he'd hurried
that one and missed again, short. After that he'd had no
choice but to go back under the arbor. And now here he
was in a standoff with a wounded man—the worst kind
of standoff, because wounded men, like wounded animals,
were a hell of a lot more dangerous.

The one advantage he had left was that the Spaniard couldn't afford to let it go on too long, play cat and mouse games with a couple of bullets in him. He'd have to either force the issue or try running away from it. If he'd already got the diamonds—and chances were he had—that might help tip the scales on the side of running.

How would he do it? Over that stone wall and through the farmland and orchards beyond? He wouldn't want to take the chance of revealing himself long enough to climb the fence; and he wouldn't be that familiar with the area—where there was another farm, where there was transportaion.

His car, the Seat on the track, was the closest and the fastest way out of here to a doctor. He couldn't know Carmody had disabled the car; he might suspect it but he couldn't know for sure. He'd risk it because it was the best choice open to him. He'd be lying over there now, thinking about the car, figuring a way to get to it from where he was. And the way he'd figure would be back along the fence until the farmyard ended and the trees began, then into the trees where there was plenty of cover and he could work his way around to the road. There was no other route he could take, except to go over the wall and he wouldn't go over the wall.

Carmody lay breathing through his mouth, watching, listening. Moon-washed darkness and bulky shadow-shapes; the fiddling of crickets, the occasional hum of a mosquito. The Spaniard was still thinking about it over there. But he'd make up his mind before long, and when he started to move Carmody would hear him. He couldn't crawl hurt over rocky ground without making some kind of noise.

When the first sounds came, four or five minutes later, they were louder than he'd expected. Leaves and branches rustling, a dragging on the ground; silence, more rustling, more dragging. Carmody strained his eyes but the blackness along the fence was impenetrable and he couldn't pinpoint the Spaniard's location by the sounds alone.

He inched backward against the farmhouse wall, until

he could no longer see the fence. Then he stood up. The rustling and dragging were still audible as he retreated to the rear corner and turned it, moving on the balls of his feet.

TUESDAY NIGHT – SILVERA

A few meters from the end of the farmyard, Silvera stopped crawling and sat with his back against the stones, his feet pulled in to one side. Sweat oiled his face, his body ... sweat and more of his own blood. The pain in his chest had grown fiery from his exertion. Already he was feeling weakened, dizzy.

He listened. At first he heard nothing; then there was a low skittering, perhaps of an unseen pebble being kicked at the far side of the clearing, beyond the grape arbor. One corner of Silvera's mouth lifted in a shark's smile. Carmody had taken the bait. Now he would go around the farmhouse and the outbuildings, into the trees on the far side of the entry road.

Silvera had thought it out carefully, putting himself in Carmody's place, in Carmody's mind. Carmody would think that escape, the services of a doctor, were his adversary's primary concern; he would think his adversary would attempt to get to his car, which Carmody had surely seen on the entry road, as quickly as possible; and he would believe that the adversary would take the safest route open to him, along the fence and then into the trees. So Silvera had made plenty of noise crawling here, so Carmody would be sure to hear him and believe that his reasoning was correct. He would not come to the fence and follow; no, that way was uncertain, left too much to chance. Instead he would go the other way, into the trees on the opposite side, and attempt an ambush at the car.

Silvera sat resting, giving Carmody time to get into the woods. But not too much time, because when no one approached the car from the opposite direction, Carmody would soon become suspicious and think of the possibility of an assault from behind. Silvera must be in position before that happened, he must stalk Carmody with great care and shoot him in the back if possible, taking care only to disable him. He had special plans for Carmody's death, oh very special plans.

One more minute passed before he heard another sound. It came from the direction of the pines, a faint crackling as of a footstep on dry pine needles. Carmody was in the woods now, moving among the trees.

Silvera pushed away from the fence, gathered his feet under him. The pain in his chest made him wince and his stance wobbly at first; then his legs steadied, and he began moving along the wall toward the farmhouse, bent low so he could not be seen above the stones. He was careful to make no sounds that could be heard more than a few feet away. His useless left arm was cradled in against his body. Sweat made the Browning slippery against his right palm.

When he came abreast of the house he paused to listen again. The crickets, nothing more. Still bent low, he ran to the side wall and laid his back against it, his breathing labored, his mouth open wide so it wouldn't be audible. The pain was savage now, feeding his hate for Carmody. And the hate gave him new strength.

He went around behind the house, half running, not worrying about sounds because the ground was thick with clay dust here. At the end of the cactus patch, he moved in along its fencing. Ahead were the outbuildings and the livestock corrals. Nothing stirred in that direction; Carmody was well into the trees by this time. He stepped out, crossed to the first of the corrals, paused a moment beside the feeding shelter there. Then he started over past the well to the second corral.

Scraping sound on rock, barely audible — and Carmody stood up behind the gallows-shaped windlass.

Silvera tried to twist and fall away, bringing the Browning up, thinking: No, you could not have known! And Carmody's first bullet tore the gun out of his hand and the second ripped into his chest, threw him sideways and down hard on his back. He lay there in the red dirt, moving his legs, only his legs, paralyzed from the waist up, looking into the bright sky overhead.

He was dying, he knew he was dying. There was terror in him as immense as the sky, so immense that he did two things he had not done since he was a boy in Esteban de Bao.

He began to cry.

And he began to pray.

TUESDAY NIGHT – CARMODY

Carmody came out from behind the well. The Spaniard was twitching on the ground, twitching and making weeping sounds—you don't twitch or cry when you're playing possum—and his weapon was lying eight feet away. But Carmody was taking no chances with the Beretta's clip empty and the nearest new one in the Porsche a long distance away. He didn't go near the man until another couple of minutes had vanished; and he didn't holster the Beretta until he got close enough to see how much blood was pumping out of the Spaniard's chest.

It had been the rustling and dragging sounds that had given him away. They'd been too loud, much too loud for a man bent on escape. Once Carmody figured them for a trick, it had been easy enough to work out what the Spaniard was really up to. So he'd made a little noise of his own, not too much, to give the impression that he'd fallen for the misdirection and was headed deep into the trees. Instead he'd doubled back here to the well and set up an ambush of his own. And the too-smart hired gun had walked right into it.

Now it was over—or almost over. Carmody picked up the man's weapon, saw that it was a Browning .380 automatic, a hell of a piece, and saw too that it was useless; the bullet he'd put into it had damaged the firing mechanism. He threw it down again, scuffed it around in the dirt with his shoe to smudge any prints he might have left. The Spaniard was still twitching, still weeping, muttering something now that was unintelligible. Carmody walked around until he found a large, heavy rock—a chunk of quartz. He took it to where the dying man lay and used it and then hurled it away into the dark.

It took only a few seconds to search the body and find the chamois pouch containing the diamonds. With the pouch in his own pocket, he crossed the yard to the farmhouse. Inside, he found the dead woman—Fanning's woman, he supposed—and when he saw her he didn't feel bad any more about using the quartz rock. He took a sheet from the bedroom, draped it over the woman to keep the flies off her blood until he could make an anonymous phone call to the Guardia Civil. Then he went out and down the lane past the Seat, walking at first and then trotting.

Gillian was locked in the Porsche, waiting for him.

WEDNESDAY,
EARLY MORNING – CARMODY

Carmody said into the telephone, "I'm calling about that information you gave me earlier tonight. There was a problem at the Hotel Mallorca Grande. Maybe you heard about it."

"I heard about it," Ibañez said. "I have details. I knew you would want them."

"Good. How serious was the attack? Fatal?"

"No, *señor*. Death would have been merciful."

"I don't follow that."

"The mind as well as the body was affected."

"The body in what way?"

"Paralysis."

"Permanent?"

"It would seem so."

"And the mind?"

"Damaged brain cells," Ibañez said, "caused by lack of oxygen. There is very little chance for recovery, the doctors say."

"Thanks. I'll be in touch."

Carmody rang off, lit one of his thin black cigars. If Miralles was a cripple and a vegetable, the diamonds belonged to him now—no contest. Give it a week, maybe two, and if Miralles' condition hadn't changed, he'd contact Van Hagen in Amsterdam and have him pick up the gems and sell them, legally or on the black market. Either way, he'd realize upwards of two hundred thousand dollars— more than enough to finance another villa and repay him for the time it would take to get set up in a new location.

He left the bedroom, saw that Gillian was still sitting huddled in one of the leather armchairs, and asked her, "How do you feel?"

She took a sip from the glass of Veterano he'd given her. "I'll be all right," she answered. Her jaw bore purplish welts and bruises where she'd been hit, and she'd complained of a headache, but it wasn't her physical state that concerned him. "It'll just take a while, that's all."

He went to the bar, poured himself a drink. Behind him Gillian said, "Will you tell me about Fernando now? What happened out there at the farm?"

It was the fourth or fifth time she'd asked him. He said the same things now he had the other times: "No. You don't want to know. You're better off forgetting any of it ever happened."

"I'll never forget it. Is he dead?"

"All right, he's not going to bother you any more."

She held the glass more tightly, looking into it as if it were a deep well and she were trying to see the bottom. She said to the glass, "I loved him once. How could I have been so wrong?"

She had said that before, too, on the ride back from the interior. Tense and frightened, she'd needed the reassurance of her own voice in the dark car and she'd kept up a running commentary. All about her relationship with Fernando Marí, and how he was the one who'd told Zaanhof about her, and what she'd felt when she recognized him last night, and the terrible way he'd been smiling, and how he had come in off the balcony and hit her with the gun. Carmody had only half-listened because none of it mattered any more, it was all past history, and he'd been thinking about Miralles and the diamonds.

Gillian lifted her head. "I was wrong about you, too, Carmody. In the beginning."

He still had nothing to say.

"You seemed cruel and uncaring about anyone but yourself. But you took my bracelet and the money from Zaanhof's villa, and you saved my life out at that farm. You do care about people, don't you? About me, just a little?"

He had no words to answer questions like that. He shrugged and said, "I took the stuff from Zaanhof's on a whim. And I had better reasons than you for going to Farm Xorrigo."

"Then you don't care anything at all about me?"

"No."

"I don't believe you."

"I don't care what you believe."

She looked at him steadily. "I'm not going home yet, with my face like it is. I think I'll stay on Majorca for a few days."

"Why tell me that?"

"Don't you want me to stay?"

"No. There's nothing for you here, on the island or in this house."

"I think there is."

Carmody was silent for a time. Then he finished his drink, put the glass down hard and went to stand in front of her. "Right now," he said, "you've got a choice. I'll drive you to a hotel in Palma Nova, or you can spend the rest of the night here. But if you stay here, you don't sleep on the sofa and you don't sleep in the spare bedroom."

"You're very blunt."

"I'm too old to play games," Carmody said. There was desire in him, deeper and more urgent than any he'd felt in a long time. And it wasn't just a need for release. There was more to Gillian Waltham than breasts and a vagina, much more—that was what had been bothering him about her all along. She had a face, she had a mind and a persona, she was real in the same way Chana had been real. He didn't want it that way but there it was; there was no sense in denying it any longer. "Well?"

"Maybe I'm being foolish again," she said softly, "but I don't care. I don't want to be alone right now. I need somebody strong . . . I need you."

He took her into the bedroom, and undressed her, and when she came into his arms she murmured against his chest, "Be gentle this first time, Carmody. I still hurt and I'm not used to sex and I've never been with a man like you. Be gentle."

He was gentle.

It was Gillian, after a while, who was not.

Pronzini
    Carmody's run

1. Books may be kept two weeks and may be
renewed twice for the same period, unless reserved.

2. A fine is charged for each day a book is not
returned according to the above rule. No book will
be issued to any person incurring such a fine until it
has been paid.

3. All injuries to books beyond reasonable wear
and all losses shall be made good to the satisfaction
of the Librarian.

4. Each borrower is held responsible for all books
charged on his card and for all fines accruing on the
same.

GAYLORD
R

MYSTERY